I0745044

C IS FOR CAPTAIN

A SIXPENNY CROSS STORY

SIXPENNY CROSS - LARGE PRINT
BOOK THREE

VICTORIA TWEAD
NEW YORK TIMES BESTSELLING AUTHOR

Ant Press
Large Print
Edition

Available in paperback, ebook and large print editions.

LARGE PRINT EDITION

Copyright © 2018, Victoria Twead

Published by AntPress.org

Ebook ISBN: 978-1-923756-03-8

Paperback ISBN: 978-1-922476-01-2

Large Print Paperback ISBN: 978-1-922476-05-0

Large Print Hardback ISBN: 978-1-923756-02-1

All rights reserved.

No part of this book may be reproduced in any form or by any electronic or mechanical means, including information storage and retrieval systems, without written permission from the author, except for the use of brief quotations in a book review.

Please note that this book, aside from recipes, is the original creation of the author. The author wrote and compiled it entirely without the use of any artificial intelligence.

USE OF THIS BOOK FOR AI TRAINING:

Without in any way limiting the author's and publisher's exclusive rights under copyright, any use of this publication to "train" generative artificial intelligence (AI) technologies to generate text is expressly prohibited. The author reserves all rights to license uses of this work for generative AI training and development of machine learning language models.

No part of this book may be reproduced in any form or by any electronic or mechanical means, including information storage and retrieval systems, without written permission from the author, except for the use of brief quotations in a book review.

CONTENTS

C IS FOR THE CAPTAIN

C IS FOR THE CAPTAIN

SIXPENNY CROSS 3

Ageing bachelors, the Captain and Sixpence, have always been inseparable. Then Babs, the new barmaid, begins work at the Dew Drop Inn.

1

Dream on, little one, and I'll put another log on the fire. I do so love to watch the orange flames flickering. Nothing is more welcoming than a real fire, so much nicer than those new-fangled electric things. It's a great pity, but nowadays not many people can be bothered with fireplaces in their homes.

If you asked me, I would say that the best fireplace in Sixpenny Cross is in the saloon of the Dew Drop Inn. I've seen the logs stacked up in the yard, higher than my shoulder. Everybody knows they can pop in and warm themselves by a blazing fire on a frosty winter's evening. The pub is hundreds of years old, and the fireplace has inglenooks on either side.

You are much too young to go in a pub, little one, and of course you won't know what an inglenook is. So I'll tell you. It's the space either side of the hearth, roomy enough for bench seats in the Dew Drop. Those seats are always occupied by regular customers. The same old faces, day after day, month after month, year after year.

Why am I telling you this? Well, I promised to tell you the story of the Captain and Sixpence, and they always sat by the fire playing dominoes, happy in each other's company. Greater friends I never saw. Nobody in Sixpenny Cross could have guessed what would happen to those two gentlemen. It's a terrible story and I'm glad you are fast asleep, little one, so you'll hear none of it.

Yes, C is for the Captain.

But wherever the Captain was, Sixpence wasn't far behind.

2

Richard Edwards, heir to Sixpenny Manor, sat at his father's bedside. The old man's life was ebbing away and there was nothing his only son could do to prevent it. He cradled his father's gnarled old hand between his own.

"The war changed all our lives," quavered the old man. "Thank God, my boy, it ended without taking you away from us."

"Yes, Father. Rest now, and try not to worry about anything."

"You know that your mother and I are very proud of you. You came out of the army an officer, a captain. I'm quite sure you would have reached a higher rank had the war continued."

"Well, thank goodness it didn't. Too many lives were lost."

Father and son lapsed into silence. The old man closed his eyes while his son watched over him. Then the dying man's eyes opened again.

"Look after your mother, Richard, she's very frail," he said.

"Of course I will, Father."

"I wish we'd given you brothers and sisters, but it wasn't to be, I'm afraid. The responsibility now is all on your shoulders."

"Don't worry, Father. Just rest."

"Son, find yourself a good woman to marry."

Father and son smiled into each other's eyes.

"I will, Father, and we'll fill this house with babies and dogs!"

"Is that a promise?"

"It is!"

His father's hand twitched once, and the smile still played on his lips as his heart finally stopped and his eyes clouded over.

The son sat motionless beside the bed, still holding his father's hand, as the bedside clock ticked the minutes away. Eventually, even his loving clasp couldn't keep the hand warm. Tears rolled down his cheeks as he bid his father a final farewell.

His mother, unable to cope with the loss of her cherished husband, soon joined him in Sixpenny Cross churchyard. Husband and wife lay side by side under the sun and stars, while their son was left to continue alone in the manor house.

It was 1951, and the Captain was thirty-one years old. A shy man at the best of times, he was discovering that being in sole charge of the manor house was too big a burden to bear.

His gregarious parents had actively participated in village events but their introverted son had avoided the limelight, preferring his own company to that of the village children. The situation was made worse when he was sent to a private boarding school, alienating him even more from the villagers.

Now, as the new squire of the manor house, his only visitor was the vicar, Thomas Ridsdale, who, having officiated at the funerals of Richard's parents, hoped their son would continue where they had left off.

"Would you care to present the prizes at this year's village fête, Captain? I'm sure the villagers would appreciate the gesture."

"I think not, Vicar," said the Captain, and the vicar didn't ask again.

Richard's days in the army had taught him how to issue orders but he didn't understand the basics of running a large house. He was awkward with the servants, and although Mrs Anderson, the housekeeper, did her best, the house did not thrive.

His father was right. He needed a wife.

And he wasn't going to find one in Sixpenny Cross.

A year had slipped by since his parents had passed away. Apart from the few remaining servants, he'd been rattling around alone in the Manor House and things needed to change. Something had to be done before it was too late. Soon, a plan began to formulate in his head.

"Mrs Anderson, I wonder if you'd mind joining me in the library in an hour. I have something rather important I wish to discuss with you," he announced one day.

"Of course, Captain."

Mrs Anderson had worked in the manor house for decades, and had known Richard since the day of his birth. Then she had addressed him as Master Richard but now, with the death of his father and as a mark of respect, addressed him as Captain.

She too had mourned the passing of the old squire, whom she had loved dearly, and now she stood in front of her employer in the library, anxious to hear what he had to say.

"Do sit down, Mrs Anderson, this won't take long."

"Thank you, Captain." Mrs Anderson perched herself on the edge of a chair and smoothed her apron.

"How is your boy, Mrs Anderson?"

The Andersons' son was actually a couple of years older than the Captain.

"We don't hear from Peter very often, sir, thank you for asking, but he's fine. When the war ended, he took a long time to find a job but he's working up north now."

"Not married?"

"No, sir. Not yet..."

The fact that the Captain, too, had not married, hung uncomfortably in the air between them.

She paused, waiting for him to continue. The Captain took a breath and resumed.

"Mrs Anderson, I've come to a decision. I've decided to live in London. I'm going to move into the family apartment in Kensington and shut this house down for the time being."

Mrs Anderson gasped, a hand flying up to cover her mouth.

"Please don't worry, Mrs Anderson! Let me explain. When I go, I'd very much like you and Mr Anderson to carry on living in the estate cottage. Of course I won't need a housekeeper any longer, but I wondered if instead, you would take on the role of caretaker? The grounds will still need looking after, so I'll still require your husband's gardening skills. His job would hardly change."

Mrs Anderson's eyes had grown large as she absorbed this information.

"I... I..."

"Of course you and Mr Anderson must have some time to think about it," the Captain hurried on, "but I would be most grateful if you would accept."

"London?" asked Anderson, shock on his face.

"Yes! If you ask me, I reckon he's going to look for a wife. He's not going to find one round here, is he?"

"And we can just carry on livin' here?"

"Yes. He said we could stay in this cottage for as long as we want. I'm to keep an eye on the house, and you're to look after the grounds and gardens like you've always done. And if the work ever gets too much for us, he'll hire some help, and if something needs fixing or mending, he'll hire somebody from the village to do that."

"Well! That sounds very decent!"

"Yes, it certainly does!"

"And how's he goin' to look after himself in London?"

"He'll go to that Gentlemen's Club to eat, the one his father was a member of."

"No, I meant financially. Will he look for work in the city?"

"No! I know for a fact he'll never need to work, his parents left him very secure. Mark my words, he won't stay in London long. Some lady will snap him up and they'll be back down here, ready to open up the house and start a family."

"You could be right. It'll be good to hear a bit of life in the old manor house again. I bet he'll be back in no time."

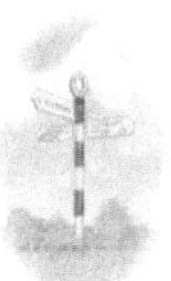

ut time marched relentlessly on.

If the Andersons thought the Captain would easily find a wife in London, they were mistaken. And if the Captain imagined he would slip effortlessly into London life, he was wrong.

The greyness of London depressed him. An all-pervading fog seemed to permanently cloak the streets, and he missed the clear air of Sixpenny Cross. He experienced the 'pea-souper' fogs he'd heard so much about and didn't enjoy them at all. Then, although the people of London were accustomed to thick fogs, worse was to come.

History was made in the December of

1952, following a spate of cold weather when folk burned more coal than usual to keep themselves warm. On a windless day, the pollution, combined with vehicle exhaust fumes, smoke from homes and industrial chimneys, was so bad, it blanketed the city.

The effects of the sulphur dioxide laden fog were deadly. At least 4,000 people died from respiratory problems, and 100,000 more were made ill. Traffic ground to a standstill because there was no visibility, and the Captain had to walk to his Club with outstretched hands, unable to see anything beyond a few feet ahead. The Great Smog of London lasted for five days. Then the weather changed and breezes arrived which swept the pollution away.

The Captain was lucky and soon shook off the cough he had acquired but the event only made him more determined to quickly find a wife and return home. He found himself staring at all females that crossed his path, wondering if any might suit his needs.

As an only child at home, then educated

in a boys' private boarding school, and finally joining the army, the Captain had had very little contact with the fairer sex. Ladies attended his parents' parties, but if any attempted to engage him in conversation, he was struck dumb with fright. He could converse well enough with male acquaintances in the Club, but as soon as they introduced him to their sisters, he became awkward and tongue-tied.

And so the years passed.

He had left the manor house entirely in the charge of Mr and Mrs Anderson, and now they were too old to do much more than potter around. When they retired to a tiny bungalow in Worthing, he paid a company to board up the manor, make it secure, and to check it regularly.

One day, he promised himself, he would go back to Sixpenny Cross. But the promise he had made to his father still ate at his soul.

It was 1964, and the Captain would soon be forty-five years old. The war had ended almost twenty years before and England was a very different place. The nation had gasped at the audacity of the Great Train Robbery, Beatlemania had swept across the country and mods and rockers were clashing at seaside resorts.

And still the Captain had not found a wife, although not for the want of trying. He'd never felt that deep emotion the Beatles sang about, the love that he knew had existed between his parents.

But he'd never stopped looking, and maybe, just maybe, he'd finally found the perfect woman in Margaret. He patted his pocket.

In his Kensington apartment, the Captain peered into the mirror, staring at his own face, trying to see it through Margaret's eyes. He wasn't a bad looking chap, he decided. Yes, his hair was beginning to silver at the temples, but nobody could call him unattractive. He turned away and pushed the curtain aside to peer out of the window onto the street below. His apartment was on the third floor, and if he craned his neck, he could see the street stretch away on either side.

Although residential, this was a busy

road, vehicles travelling faster than they should. Two businessmen wearing long coats and bowler hats walked together. Each carried a rolled up newspaper and an umbrella. A beggar sat on the pavement, leaning against the railings. He lifted his hand hopefully, palm upwards, as the men approached, but he might as well have been invisible. The men hardly slowed their pace as they skirted round him.

A street cleaner trundled his cart up the road, and this time the beggar didn't even lift his head.

A black taxi cab rounded the corner, and the Captain's heart gave a little lurch.

Margaret!

The Captain bounded down the communal stairs and walked out into the street just as the cab driver drew up. The rear window was wound down, framing Margaret's pretty face.

"Richard!"

"Hello, Margaret, shall I hold the driver, or pay him off?"

"Oh, pay him, I think."

Margaret watched as the Captain paid

her fare, then opened her door. She stepped out onto the pavement, and straightened. The taxi drew away to join the stream of traffic, leaving them alone.

"Margaret, you look wonderful, as usual."

"Thank you, Richard."

If her voice sounded a little flat, and her eyes avoided his, he didn't notice.

He kissed her proffered cheek, enjoying the scent of jasmine that always accompanied her.

"I thought I'd take you to a new restaurant for lunch. Are you hungry?"

"That sounds super, Richard, but do you think we could just go for a stroll?"

"Of course, shall we head towards the Gardens? We can always hail a cab to the restaurant from there."

"Good idea."

It wasn't far to the park and they walked together, side by side. Margaret was unusually quiet and the Captain couldn't think of a word to say. The little square ring box was burning a hole in his pocket as he silently rehearsed his script.

I'll ask her at the park, he thought, *when it feels right. Or perhaps I should wait until we get to the restaurant? I'll make sure we have the best table. Should I kneel? No! Perhaps I'll wait until we are quite alone, somewhere else, another day…*

The Captain used the busy road as an excuse to hold her arm as he found a safe gap between the passing traffic. He guided her across, but when they reached the other side, Margaret pulled away from his grasp.

Ah, she's such an independent soul, he thought to himself. *Father would approve of that.*

"It's a pity we didn't bring bread for the swans," said Margaret, breaking into the Captain's thoughts. "Shall we sit here at this bench, for a while?"

"Of course."

They sat side by side, facing the water, watching the swans dip their long necks into the water. Their view was interrupted for a moment by a mother pushing a high baby carriage in front of them. The infant seated in the pram regarded the pair on the bench without expression.

Shall I ask her now? he thought, and his

hand started snaking towards his pocket. *Is now the right time?*

"Richard, I've been meaning to talk to you," said Margaret.

"Oh, Margaret, I've been meaning to talk to you, too!"

He reached for her hand, and she allowed him to hold it. The Captain took this as a good sign and his heart swelled.

"Oh dear, I'm afraid you may not like what I am about to say," said Margaret, looking into his face properly for the first time that day.

4

Something icy gripped the Captain's heart. He stared at the lady by his side, desperately trying to read her expression but failing miserably.

"I'm so sorry, Richard, but I don't think it's going to work."

A pair of mallards swam into view and a swan stretched up to flap its wings.

"What? What isn't going to work?" He gripped her hand tighter, but she pulled it free.

"Us, Richard. You and me. I'm terribly sorry. I care for you, of course, but I don't feel we were made to be together..."

The Captain felt cold, almost detached.

This wasn't what he'd planned. This wasn't how it was supposed to be.

"But you care for me?" he said at last.

"Yes, but not in *that* way, if you know what I mean…"

"But perhaps you could, in the future…"

"No, Richard. I'm sorry. I didn't want to tell you, but I've met somebody else…"

He gaped at her.

"Richard, you must let me go. Please don't be sad, and I know you'll meet another nice girl very soon. I'm so sorry, but there was no easy way to tell you."

She was standing. She leaned down and patted his arm, then turned and swung away up the path.

"Margaret!"

But she didn't respond.

Numb, he watched her receding figure disappear behind some ornamental trees. When he lost sight of her, all hope died.

"I bought you a ring," he whispered, "I was going to ask you to marry me."

And then the world seemed to collapse around him. He stumbled to his feet and lurched back along the path the way they had come.

"Oy!" said a man jumping out of his way. "Watch out!"

But the Captain was blind to his surroundings.

Margaret doesn't want to be my wife.

Margaret has gone.

He staggered across the road, ignoring the honking from irate drivers.

"'Ere mate, look where yer bleedin' going!" yelled a taxi driver, shaking his fist.

But the Captain heard nothing. All he wanted to do was reach home, close the curtains and sit alone in the dark to lick his wounds. Miraculously, no vehicle mowed him down and he reached the other side safely.

Home was within sight, just one more street to cross.

Looking neither left nor right, he stepped into the road.

Kevin Stephens' knuckles were white as he gripped the steering wheel. He was late. He was supposed to pick up his wife from the corner of Kensington High Street twenty minutes ago, and Lynn Stephens didn't like being kept waiting. If Lynn was annoyed, she could sulk for England.

If he took a shortcut, and kept his foot heavy on the pedal, he might get away with it. He'd tell her that he'd been delayed because he'd been in a travel agency, looking at booking one of those new package holidays to Spain she was always harping on about. Or he'd suggest they go to the pictures, maybe see that new film, *A Hard Day's Night*, starring those long-haired layabouts she liked so much. Kevin glanced at his watch.

It all happened in a split second.

He never saw the man step out into the road in front of him.

Just as the Captain stepped forward, a small figure materialised from nowhere, grabbing the Captain's coat and yanking him backwards. The corner of the car's bumper made contact with the Captain's right leg as he fell back into the arms of his saviour.

Kevin slammed on his brakes and screeched to a stop. As the smartly-dressed man and the beggar slowly extricated themselves and stood up, he exhaled, realising that nobody was hurt.

"You bloody idiot!" he yelled at the Captain with a mixture of anger and fright, "I nearly ran you over! If it hadn't been for that bloke jumping in, you'd have been a goner!"

Shaking his head, a relieved Kevin drove off. At least now he had an excuse for Lynn. Perhaps he might embellish the story just a little bit...

The Captain gaped at the man who was still supporting him, guiding him back to the pavement and safety.

"You saved my life," he said.

"It was just luck," said the beggar. "I happened to see you walkin' down the street, and I could see you were a bit distracted, like. So when you walked out into the road, I only had to grab you. Are you hurt at all?"

"No, just bruised, I think…" The Captain rubbed his shin and looked ruefully at his torn trouser leg. "But if it hadn't been for you, it would have been much worse."

"Oh, it was just a bit of luck. Anyway, that driver was goin' much too fast."

"Well, I can't thank you enough. Let me shake your hand!"

The two men shook hands, one manicured, the other grimy with torn fingernails.

"If you hadn't grabbed me, I think I'd have died under the wheels of that motor. I live just over there, will you come in? I think we could both do with a drink to get over the shock."

"Well, sir, if you're sure…"

"Oh yes, I'm very sure! And I daresay I could rustle up something to eat, too, if you fancy it."

The beggar grinned from ear to ear.

"Just one thing, sir, would you mind if I asked you a question?"

"Of course not! Fire away!"

"Forgive me if I've got it wrong, sir, it's been a few years," said the beggar, "but is your name Richard, by any chance? Richard Edwards from Sixpenny Cross?"

The Captain gaped at the beggar, then stared closer at the slight figure in front of him. He looked past the ten-day stubble and the tattered scarf wound round the neck, past the unkempt hair and torn clothing.

"Good Lord!" he exclaimed, his mouth hanging open. "Mr and Mrs Anderson's boy!"

"Well, hardly a boy, sir," said the beggar, smiling. "I'm actually two years older than you. But yes, I was born in the cottage in the grounds of Sixpenny Manor."

"Well! Good gracious! What a coincidence! Come along, old man, let's drink to this! We've got a lot to talk about!"

The Captain clapped Peter Anderson on the back, and the pair made their way up to the Captain's apartment.

Much later, the street cleaner trundled his cart back down the road, when something in the gutter caught his eye. He bent down, squinting. It was a small, velvet-covered box, the kind used by jewellers to display rings. Looking left and right to check he wasn't being observed, he picked it up and cracked it open. A flash from the diamond inside was enough for him to slip the box quickly into his pocket and hurry away.

"Finders, keepers," he muttered.

It was his lucky day.

5

Upstairs in the Captain's apartment, the two men sat in armchairs, a decanter of whiskey on the table between them.

"It's Peter, isn't it?" asked the Captain, suddenly recalling their housekeeper and gardener's son's name.

"Yes, that's right, sir, but nobody calls me that."

"They don't? So what do they call you?"

"Well, don't laugh, sir, but everybody calls me Sixpence, on account of my size, and where I come from."

"Then I shall call you Sixpence, too," decided the Captain. "And nobody calls me

Richard, either. They all know me as the Captain. A relic of the war, of course."

Peter Anderson had indeed begun life in the grounds of the manor house in Sixpenny Cross. His parents had met because his mother was employed as a maid, and his father worked in the gardens. The pair had married and a party was held in the servants' hall to celebrate. The happy couple were presented with an estate cottage, and two years later, Peter was born.

Mrs Anderson went on to become housekeeper, and Peter's father was promoted to chief groundsman. Peter, although not naturally academic, went to school in Sixpenny Cross, and later he attended a school in Yewbridge.

The housekeeper's son, Peter, and Richard Edwards, the squire's son, were similar in age, but their paths seldom crossed. They belonged to different social classes.

"So what did you do when you left school?" the Captain wanted to know. "I don't remember seeing you at Sixpenny Cross. And how did you come to be, er, on the streets of Kensington?" He had avoided the word 'begging' but they both knew that's what he meant. "I assume, Sixpence, that things lately haven't been too prosperous for you?"

"You could say that, sir."

"Have you been in contact with your parents? I understand that they are living in Worthing now."

Peter shifted uneasily in his armchair.

"I'd rather not, sir, seeing as how things have been with me. I don't want to worry them."

Sixpence had devoured a thick gentlemen's relish sandwich that the Captain had prepared for him, and the delicious taste of anchovies was still on his tongue. Now the whiskey warmed him, and he was ready to talk.

"When I left school, I became apprenticed to a builder in Yewbridge. Didn't like it much, to be honest. I was pretty happy to be accepted into the army when the war broke out."

"You were in the army, too?"

"I was. Only a Private."

"Did you see action?"

"I did." Sixpence smiled ruefully. "If I'd known how hard it was going to be, I doubt I'd have volunteered so quickly."

The Captain nodded. Life hadn't been easy for any soldiers in the second world war. But to have been a Private would have been very hard, compared with that of an officer like himself.

"And I wouldn't have lost my fingers."

Sixpence held his hand up, revealing three missing fingers, a fact that the Captain had failed to notice until now.

"What happened to them?"

"Blown away by a mine."

"And when the war ended, what did you do then?"

"Oh this and that. So many houses needed rebuildin' after the bombing, I thought I'd pick up work easy. But I couldn't go back to the buildin' trade, not with no fingers, nobody would employ me. So I had to think again. I was a caretaker in a school in north London for quite a few years until the council took over and changed things. I worked for a while as a petrol attendant and then I had a stroke of luck. I got chattin' with one of the regulars at the petrol station, and he offered me a live-in job as caretaker at his block of flats in Battersea. I jumped at that, I can tell you!"

"So what happened?"

"It was fine for a few years until the old boy, the owner of the flats, passed away. Soon as he was laid in the ground, his relatives were swarmin' all over the building, givin' tenants their notice and makin' plans about what they were goin' to do with the place. They couldn't give me my notice fast enough. I got into an argument about it, and they refused to give me a reference. Believe me, you can't get a job without a reference nowadays. So that's why I ended up on the streets."

The Captain shook his head in disbelief. How many times had he passed Sixpence, and never even really seen him, let alone offered any help?

"You never married?" he asked.

"No, sir. Never felt I found the right girl, and never felt I had anything to offer a wife, anyway. What about you, sir? Was that your wife I saw you with earlier today?"

The Captain started. He had forgotten all about the painful break up with Margaret. He patted his pocket, and was surprised to discover that the ring box was gone. Curiously, he felt no sense of loss.

"No, she was just, er, a friend," he said. "I never married."

"Righty-ho," said Sixpence, and took another sip of whiskey.

The Captain's leg was throbbing painfully reminding him how close his brush with death, or very serious injury, had been.

"I want to demonstrate my thanks to you for saving my life today," he said. "Would you accept a sum of money?"

Sixpence looked affronted.

"No, of course not, sir. I told you, it was just luck that I was there. Anybody would have done the same thing."

"Well, at least stay here in my apartment for a few days. As long as you like. Until you get back on your feet."

"That's very kind, sir, but I don't think

so. It wouldn't be right. I wouldn't be comfortable doin' that."

"But I want to help you, old man. If it hadn't been for you, I'd be in Westminster hospital, or maybe even some morgue, by now."

Sixpence shrugged and took another sip of whiskey.

"Well, thank you, but I'm afraid the only thing I really need is a job," he said.

The two men sat in silence, Sixpence enjoying the rare comforts, while the Captain thought hard.

Suddenly, it came to him in a flash of clarity.

"I've got it!" he said, setting down his glass and almost spilling it in his haste. "How would you feel about going back to Sixpenny Cross?"

6

*S*ixpence stared at his companion.

"How do you mean, sir?"

"It just struck me that I've had enough of London, and I want to go home. I want to go back to Sixpenny Manor."

Sixpence was listening hard.

"Don't you see? The house has been shut for years. In fact it's boarded up. Your parents have retired to Worthing and I need you to help me get it all opened up again. Nobody has lived in it for years."

"A job?"

"Yes, we'll need to get the electricity and water connected again. And reconnect the telephone. The place will be frightfully dusty and will probably need to be cleaned thoroughly. We can get help from the village, of course."

"We'll have to check the roof tiles and windows for storm damage," said Sixpence, beginning to become infected by the Captain's enthusiasm. "And check the oak panellin' and furniture for woodworm."

"Exactly! And goodness knows what the grounds are like! You can see I'll need a man like yourself to help me straighten it all up."

Sixpence's eyes danced as he stared back at the Captain. Then he sobered.

"And when the house is comfortable again, what then?"

"Well, let's see how we rub along together," said the Captain. "We can discuss it more later, but I imagine I'll still need some help. If it all goes well, I think I'd like you to stay on as my companion, if you will. Can you cook at all, by any chance?"

"Yes, I enjoy cookin'. Just plain food, mind, not fancy stuff."

"Well, you saw what a mess I made of your sandwich earlier, and that's about the only thing I know how to prepare. I wouldn't expect you to do much, just a meal now and then."

Sixpence was beaming.

"So what do you say, old man, will you accept the job?"

"Thank you, sir, I will."

For the second time that day, the Captain shook Sixpence's hand.

Over the weeks that followed, the two men set to work breathing life back into the manor. The Captain visited Jayne Fairweather, the postmistress and owner of Sixpenny Cross's only general store, who provided him with the details of local tradesmen.

They employed painters and carpenters, glaziers and roofers. They replaced the ancient fridge in the kitchen, and added a new electric cooker, which soon became Sixpence's pride and joy. They had linoleum laid, as well as acres of new carpet. They bought a Persian rug and a black-and-white television set for the drawing room.

When the house was finished, they settled down to a quiet life, and soon fell into a comfortable routine that would continue for years. The Captain read his newspapers, wrote letters, paid bills and sometimes took a walk in the grounds. Sixpence carried out household duties. A keen gardener, he used any spare time to tend his beloved roses. The Captain employed outside help to look after the extensive grounds, but the roses and kitchen garden were Sixpence's domain.

Every evening, after dinner, the pair would walk to the Dew Drop Inn and sit in the inglenook. The pub landlord, Angus McDonald, always left the battered old box of dominoes on the table. The pair would play a few games, drink two pints of beer, then return home to retire to bed.

And so the years slipped by.

Neither man had found a wife to share his life, but they were content enough in each other's company.

Now it was March, 1985. The devastating, year-long miners' strike had just ended and a debate in the House of Lords had been televised for the first time.

The Captain smiled, remembering the black-and-white TV set he and Sixpence had purchased back in 1964, when they'd first returned from London with such enthusiasm to open Sixpenny Manor. His mind drifted back even further, to the 1950s, when the house had buzzed and he was a young man with his life ahead of him.

Visions of the manor house in the old days played in the Captain's head. When his parents had been alive, the house had throbbed with life. Servants, ruled by Mrs Anderson, the housekeeper, kept the rooms clean and tidy. The family had a resident cook then, and the kitchen smelled of baking bread and roast meat.

During those years after the war ended, the country was gripped by a kind of forced gaiety. The wireless was usually left switched on to the BBC's Light Entertainment Programme, and comedy shows like Max Bygraves's *Educating Archie* filled the drawing room with canned laughter.

His mother had held cocktail parties, soirées and seasonal balls. His father hosted shooting parties. On those days, the boot boy, the gardener and the gardener's boy were employed as beaters for the day. Their job was to scare the game birds out of the thickets and into the path of the huntsmen. The men returned, victoriously brandishing braces of pheasants that were thrown onto the kitchen table. Later, the pheasants, or trout from the river, would be served up on silver platters.

In those days they had labradors, dogs that slept under tables or in front of the fire, but barked when visitors' cars swept up the gravel drive.

The Captain gazed up at his father's portrait. His father leaned on a shooting stick, a slight smile on his healthy, sun-reddened face, the light catching his slightly bulbous nose, so like his son's. When the portrait was painted, his father must have been in his forties. His hair, already receding, was beginning to silver. The

Captain had inherited the same trait. Now, in his sixties, the Captain's own hair was sparse and almost white.

What would Father say if he could see the manor house now? the Captain wondered.

"Well, I've given your old Dad a good dusting, Captain," said Sixpence, breaking into the Captain's thoughts. "Amazin' how these old portraits attract the dust."

"Thank you, Sixpence. You are a good man. I often wonder how I'd manage in this big old house without you."

"It's a pleasure, sir. You've given me a roof over my head for more years than I care to remember."

The Captain smiled and looked back at his newspaper.

When the Captain and Sixpence had first moved back to Sixpenny Cross, they'd thrown themselves into opening up the house again, but it was soon apparent that most of the rooms would never be used. They rarely had visitors, and the large, empty house proved too much for Sixpence to maintain.

Gradually, over the years, he and Sixpence

had closed off unused rooms, covering the furniture with dust sheets. The dining hall that used to ring with witty conversation and the sound of laughter was locked and rarely visited. The library was shut, its books seldom read. Tapping heels no longer waltzed on the parquet dance floor, and the grand piano was silent. Most of the bedrooms were shrouded and dark, the heavy drapes remaining drawn year after year.

No chatter emanated from the kitchen, and the only dishes that ever cooled on the counters were plain fare prepared by Sixpence.

What need did two old men have for all those rooms? Apart from the kitchen, and a bedroom and bathroom each, they only required a room to sit in, to while away the long hours in each other's company. In summer and winter they sat in the overstuffed armchairs of the drawing room.

Long ago, the Captain had asked Sixpence to pack away most of the ornaments that decorated the side tables, mantlepiece and all available surfaces.

"We've no need for all those things," he had said, with a sweep of his arm, indicating the buddhas, carved antelopes and tigers his grandfather had brought back from India a lifetime ago.

"All of 'em, sir?" Sixpence had asked.

"Yes, they're just dust traps. No need for all that clutter."

"Well, I won't argue with that," Sixpence had replied.

"And get rid of the old wireless, it hasn't worked for years."

"Very good, sir."

"And I know my mother loved all that cut glass and crystal, but I've never been very fond of it. It can all be packed away, except perhaps the carved elephant on the hall stand. Mother said it brought the house luck."

"Right you are, sir."

"And leave a few vases? I do enjoy seeing the roses you grow, Sixpence."

Sixpence had beamed. He had inherited his love of gardening from his own father, and over the years, the manor's roses and kitchen garden had flourished under his care.

"Most of the paintings can go, too." The Captain's eyes had swept round the room, taking in the hunting scenes and seascapes that adorned the walls. "Just leave the portraits of my father and mother, either side of the fireplace, and maybe that Indian scimitar. I've always rather liked that."

When the paintings had been removed, rectangles marked the wallpaper where they had hung for decades.

"Well, I'm off to grill us a couple of nice pork chops," said Sixpence, snapping the Captain back to the present. "Dinner will be in about half an hour. Then we'll toddle off to the Dew Drop as usual, shall we?"

"Yes, thank you. Let me know if you need any help with the dinner."

"Ta, I will."

But they both knew Sixpence would never ask for the Captain's help. He prided himself in caring for his friend and benefactor.

The Captain gazed at his parents' portraits, then shut his eyes, dozing.

The lights blazed in the Dew Drop Inn even though the landlord, Angus McDonald, hadn't yet unlocked the doors. Opening time was in twenty minutes and there was still a lot to do.

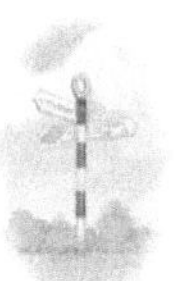

7

Angus McDonald watched carefully as the woman pulled the handle slowly towards herself. Dark beer poured into the glass until it almost reached the rim. Before the white froth overflowed, she stopped, then looked at him sideways.

"Well?"

"Well, I must say, Barbara, you managed that pump with no trouble," he said. "That's a perfect pint you've pulled there. I can see you've had plenty of bar experience."

"Oh, I'd love a penny for every pint of ale I've drawn over the years! It's like second nature to me." She threw back her head and laughed. Then she looked at him coyly and winked. "And call me Babs, nobody ever calls me Barbara."

"Good! And you're quite happy handling the till?"

"Of course." She folded her arms confidently over her ample bosom.

"Right then, Babs, you familiarise yourself with the optics, and the different types of glasses. And could you check the Ladies' and Gents' rooms, please? I'm going to bring in some more wood and stoke up the fire. It's another cold night, and our regulars always expect a good fire to warm themselves."

Yes, he thought as he tended the fire. *I think I made a good choice with Babs. She's not in her first flush of youth, and she's a bit, er, loud, but she seems capable. She's an experienced barmaid and customers like to see a cheerful face behind the bar.*

When he'd placed the advertisement for bar staff in the Yewbridge Gazette, a handful of applicants had responded, but only Babs had worked in a bar before. He'd offered her the job, and he was pleased with his choice so far. True, everything about Babs seemed a little exaggerated. Her laugh was a little too loud, her skirt a little too short, especially for a lady her age, and her top was a little too plunging. But nothing too serious. She *was* a barmaid after all.

"Right, time to open up," he said, glancing at his watch.

He slid open the two bolts on the front door and returned to stand beside Babs behind the bar.

"Tell me about the regulars," she said. "Always good to know a bit about the clientele."

"Well, Stan Cooper often drops in for a pint after work. He's the village policeman."

"I bet there's not much crime here in Sixpenny Cross!"

"No, you're quite right. The Tait's cottage down the street burnt down a while ago, but that was an electrical fault, they think. Actually, you might meet Bella Tait. She pops in sometimes to see Scout here." He stroked the cat curled up on the counter. "I adopted him from her when she used to rescue animals."

"Anyone else?"

"There's Archie Draper, he's got the farm near Sixpenny Woods. And Simon and Daisy Granger. Oh, and of course there's the Captain and Sixpence…"

Babs went off into a peal of laughter.

"Who? The Captain and Sixpence?"

"Yes. The Captain owns Sixpenny Manor. Sixpence is his companion and lives with him. They come in every evening and sit by the fire and play dominoes."

"They're not married?"

"No, they live alone. The Captain is a simple sort, but Sixpence looks after him. Ssh, here they are."

The pub door was pushed open, and two men entered, one tall and well-built, the other short and angular.

"Evening, Captain, evening, Sixpence," called Angus. "Cold out there tonight, isn't it?"

"It is," agreed the Captain, as he and Sixpence hung their hats and scarves on the rack beside the door.

"Never mind, spring is comin'," said Sixpence cheerfully. "The daffodils are ready to open and warmer weather will soon be here.”

“Can’t wait! I’m tired of these winter clothes,” said Babs, laughing as though she had made a joke.

Both the Captain and Sixpence swung round, noticing the owner of the voice for the first time. Sixpence gave Babs an easy smile, while the Captain’s eyebrows shot up in surprise.

“This is Babs Mason, my new barmaid,” said Angus. “I’ll send her over with a pint of your usual in just a moment, and you can meet her properly.”

The Captain and Sixpence settled down in their customary corner, without speaking. Sixpence overturned the waiting wooden box and spilled the dominoes onto the table in readiness for a game.

“Good fire tonight,” he remarked.

But the Captain didn’t hear him. He was staring over Sixpence’s shoulder, his gaze drawn to the buxom woman behind the bar as she loaded a tray with two pints of beer. She probably sensed his eyes upon her and looked up from her task. One of her heavily painted eyelids lowered and rewarded the Captain with an exaggerated wink.

The Captain shivered very slightly, and Sixpence caught the movement.

"You alright, sir?" he asked.

"Yes, yes. Perfectly okay thank you."

Babs had reached the table with her tray.

"Here you are, gentlemen," she said, a broad smile on her face. She placed a pint in front of each man, bending low enough for both men to view her ample cleavage.

"Thank you, and very pleased to meet you," said Sixpence extending his hand to shake. "They call me Sixpence."

"Oh!" said Babs, seizing his hand, "and what did they call you when you were a nipper, Threepence?" She threw her head back and laughed at her own joke.

"Very good," said Sixpence, smiling politely and reclaiming his hand.

Babs turned to his companion.

"And you must be the Captain."

But the Captain had been struck completely dumb.

"My name's Babs, but you know that already." Another peal of laughter. "Well, good to make your acquaintance, gentlemen. Just let me know when you're ready for another pint and I'll be right over."

She made her way back to the bar as Sixpence laid all the dominoes face down on the table. He selected seven of them for himself. Although appearing to be busy, he was very aware that the Captain was unsettled. He waited.

"What a creature..." said the Captain, shaking his head.

"Babs? Oh, typical barmaid type, I'd say."

"Do you think so?"

"Yes, I think she'll be a real asset to the Dew Drop, probably cheer the place up."

The Captain said no more and selected his own seven dominoes.

The door swung open, admitting more thirsty customers. Angus and Babs were kept busy pouring drinks as the two men played dominoes. At regular intervals Babs's raucous laugh would fill the saloon and the Captain's eyes would flicker in the direction of the bar again.

"Are you ready for another pint?" asked

Sixpence when he'd won five easy games in a row and both their glasses were drained.

The Captain nodded.

"I'll order them on my way to the cloakroom," said Sixpence, standing.

The pub was fairly busy now, but he managed to attract Babs's attention and signal for another two pints as he passed the counter. Babs poured the beer quickly, and, to the Captain's horror, began making her way to his table.

"There you go, Captain," she said.

"Thank you, Barbara," he managed.

She leaned down low in front of him to plonk the glasses on the table. He tried very hard not to look at the secret flesh she was revealing, but failed. Her perfume reached his nostrils and he almost stopped breathing.

"Well, Captain," she said, looking straight into his face, close enough for him to feel her hot breath, "you just let me know if you need anything else."

The Captain was lost.

8

"Are you quite sure you don't want to go to the pub, sir?" asked Sixpence.

It was extremely rare for the Captain and Sixpence to miss their evening walk to the pub, but the Captain was adamant; he didn't want to go.

As Sixpence cleared away the dinner plates and tidied the kitchen, he tried to figure out the cause of the Captain's refusal.

If I didn't know better, he thought to himself, *I reckon it's got somethin' to do with that new barmaid, Babs.*

He shook his head, concerned.

Meanwhile, the Captain sat in the

drawing room, replaying the events of last evening over and over again.

Barbara.

First that wink.

What did it mean? Why had she singled him out and winked at him in such a familiar way?

And then, *you just let me know if you need anything else. What did she mean by that?* He remembered her hot breath on his face and felt his palms sweating.

"I'll find us somethin' nice to watch on the TV," said Sixpence, fiddling with the dials. "Won't do us any harm to miss a night at the pub."

The Captain watched the flickering screen but absorbed nothing.

When he retired to bed he struggled to sleep for a second night. Owls hooted in Sixpenny Woods and the moon travelled slowly across the sky. The Captain tossed and turned, but every time he closed his eyes, Barbara's painted face floated in front of him.

You just let me know if you need anything else, the vision whispered, and in slow motion, one eyelid lowered in a suggestive wink.

The next day saw a clear sky and the air felt warmer than it had for months. The hedgerows were alive with songbirds, and the ducks on the village green were building nests.

After breakfast, Sixpence visited his rose garden. He smiled at the neat rows of rose bushes before examining the new buds for any sign of insect or fungus attack. The bushes, severely pruned for the winter but now bursting with vigorous growth, looked the picture of health.

"Well," said Sixpence, "with a bit of luck, they'll win me some more First Place rosettes at the fête in June."

The Captain, too, was feeling more positive with the new day. He had come to a decision. He would brood no more about the barmaid. He would accompany Sixpence to the pub that evening, just as they always did, and he would ignore her. He must have imagined her interest in him. Why would a woman like that take a special interest in him?

Of course, if she made another move, then he would reconsider.

When Yewbridge Town Council handed over the flat to its latest tenants, the walls had been painted a fresh magnolia. Now the walls were nicotine-stained and the rooms stank of stale cigarettes and smoke. Hardly surprising, as the occupants were rarely without a cigarette between their fingers and the windows were seldom opened.

Husband and wife sat side by side on a sofa covered with a grubby blanket, their feet up on a shared vinyl pouffe. The man was leafing through *The Sun* newspaper, staring awhile at the topless pin-up girl on page three.

"Don't know why you're gawking at her, Rick," exclaimed the woman, "she must be half your age."

She went back to examining her own face in a hand-held mirror.

"Well, I can look, can't I?" he replied, before glancing at the news stories. "Still can't believe we have a woman for prime minister," he growled. "Gawd, that Maggie Thatcher should never be allowed to run the country."

His wife didn't reply, she'd heard it many times before.

"Would you look at this! A blooming Egyptian has bought Harrods! *Mohammed Al Fayed buys Harrods*. Whatever next! Probably sell Buckingham Palace to the Americans next."

"Why should you care?" asked the woman. "You've never been into Harrods once in your life."

"It's the principle of the thing," he said, stubbing out his cigarette in the overflowing ashtray between them.

"Hey, who knows," said Babs. "Maybe we'll be able to afford to shop in Harrods too, some day, what with my new job going so well. Which reminds me, my roots need seeing to. Gotta look my best now that I'm working."

The woman who sat on the sofa beside her husband in that dingy Yewbridge flat bore no resemblance to the Dew Drop's new barmaid. Gone were the stockings and high heels. Instead, Babs's thick white legs were bare and pushed into grimy slippers that may have been pink once. The short skirt and plunging blouse that had so caught the Captain's eye hung from a coat-hanger hooked onto the picture rail that ran around the room. Now Babs wore a faded, floral, quilted dressing-gown that gaped between the button holes, revealing patches of dimpled grey flesh. Her face, devoid of make-up, was blotched and her eyes were small and unremarkable.

She drew out a pack of cigarettes from her dressing-gown pocket, selected one and put it between her lips before lighting it and inhaling deeply. She belched comfortably.

"Let's have a few beers tonight, Rick," she suggested, "and then get ourselves a takeaway pizza. Might as well enjoy my night off."

"Can I pour anybody another coffee?" asked Sara Ridsdale, the vicar's wife, looking round the table.

Everybody politely refused.

The organisers of the annual Sixpenny Cross fête were attending a meeting in the vicarage. The vicar, Thomas Ridsdale, was checking his notes.

"Well, I think we have everything covered. The marquees have been booked. Jayne, you'll get the flyers printed?"

Jayne Fairweather nodded. "I'll keep a stack in the Post Office to give out, and I'll make sure they're pasted on lamp posts and different spots closer to the time. I'll also get the certificates printed for the home produce competitions and the flower arrangements. I'll organise the entries, too, if you like."

"Jayne, you're a marvel," smiled the vicar. "Daisy, are you happy to run the cake stall again?"

"No problem, vicar, I'll get some

volunteers to bake for it, too. And I'm sure Abigail Martin will help out on the day."

"I'll bake some cakes," said Emily Draper, the farmer's wife.

"And Simon, you and Archie did a wonderful job last year, sorting the trestle tables and the stalls on the day. Are you happy to do that again?"

Simon Grainger and Archie Draper both nodded.

"Stan, raffle?"

The policeman nodded.

And so the meeting progressed as it had done every year for generations.

"Well, I think we have all the basics covered," said the vicar, closing his notebook. "We have more than two months to prepare, lots of time, hopefully, although we always seem to be in a panic at the end. Put your thinking caps on for next week's meeting, and we'll make a list of stalls and who to ask to run them."

He stood and the meeting broke up amidst a buzz of chatter. Some headed home, others for a quick drink at the Dew Drop.

At the same time, the Captain and Sixpence were also preparing to visit the pub.

9

The Dew Drop Inn was often busy on a Sunday evening, and tonight it was busier than usual. When the Captain and Sixpence arrived, the bar was crowded with people.

"Evening, Captain, evening, Sixpence," called Angus McDonald. "Sit yourselves down and I'll be right over."

"Good evening, Captain, hello, Sixpence, were your ears burning?" asked Jayne Fairweather, smiling, as the two men passed her on their way to the inglenook seats.

"Hello, Jayne, ears burnin'? No, why?" answered Sixpence.

The Captain said nothing. His eyes and

ears were searching and listening for any sight or sound of Babs's presence in the pub. His hands were shaking.

"Well, we were just wondering how your roses are coming along this year and whether you were going to walk away with all the first prizes at the fête again. We had a fête meeting at the vicarage this evening."

"Ah! That explains why the pub's so busy tonight," said Sixpence, grinning. "I have to say, I'm pretty pleased with my rose bushes so far, thank you for askin', but it's early days. A lot can go wrong in two months. Next year I'm going to have a go at chrysanthemums, too, so look out!"

"I'll never enter my roses in the village fête, but I wish they grew better than they do. Have you any tips for me?"

"Bananas," said Sixpence, lowering his tone. "Chop up banana skins and spread them round the base. Roses love the potassium, you see. We always save our banana skins for the roses. Isn't that right, Captain?"

But the Captain had already taken his seat in the inglenook.

"I can see you're rushed off your feet," said Sixpence, catching sight of Angus bringing their beers. "I'll take those off your hands."

"Thanks, mate. It's Babs's night off, and I'm a bit pushed."

Sixpence joined his companion in the inglenook and set down their drinks.

"Poor old Angus has his work cut out tonight," he remarked. "It's the new barmaid's night off."

He saw the Captain's shoulders tense, then relax.

I was right, thought Sixpence. *He's got that wretched woman on the brain.*

Unfortunately, Sixpence's suspicions were correct. The Captain's simple nature had a tendency to obsess, much like a child's. The barmaid occupied his mind entirely, leaving little space for anything else.

The next night, when they arrived at the pub, the Captain managed to greet Babs civilly and he tried hard not to watch her as she worked. Although determined to ignore her, his intentions were thrown to the wind by a tiny incident that anyone else might have brushed aside as meaningless.

Early in the evening, while they were engrossed in a game of dominoes, Babs approached unnoticed from behind.

"Well, gentlemen," she said, standing between them and laying a hand on each of their shoulders, one broad, one bony.

The Captain nearly jumped out of his skin, and the hand on his shoulder felt as hot as a cattle brand.

"Who's going to buy me a drink, then?" she wheedled. "It's gone quiet, and I'm spitting feathers."

"Please pour yourself anything you like, Barbara," he said, "and put it on my bill."

"Thank you kindly, Captain," she replied, laughing loudly and leaving her hand on his shoulder for just a little too long. "I'll do that and come right back and enjoy it with you. I'm due a break."

"Well, actually, we're just..." said Sixpence.

"You are very welcome, my dear," cut in the Captain, giving Sixpence an icy look.

True to her word, Babs returned and sat

with the two men. She hung on every word the Captain uttered and her raucous laugh rang round the pub.

When they walked home that night, the Captain's heart was beating faster.

He *wasn't* mistaken.

Barbara *had* taken a shine to him.

Beside him, Sixpence said nothing, but he was worried.

That evening set the pattern for future weeks. Every day, the Captain would occupy himself with writing letters, paying bills, or walking round the grounds, but he was whiling away the hours until he could return to the pub and see Babs. Sixpence cooked and carried out his duties as usual, but as he tended his roses in the walled garden, he worried.

Every evening, the Captain and Sixpence would take their seats in the pub and begin to play dominoes. Then the Captain would buy Babs a drink, often more. She'd pour herself a generous gin and tonic then join the two men in the inglenook. Dominoes forgotten, the Captain beamed and went pink whenever she laid her hand on his arm to emphasise a point.

Gradually, Sixpence detached himself. He'd make excuses and linger at the bar, chatting with other customers, and when the two men walked home, it was often in silence.

———

"I tell you," said Babs to her husband, "I reckon I've got the Captain eating out of my hand. The old goat's got the hots for me!"

They both laughed uproariously.

"Well," said Rick, "you ought to put it to some use. We've got bills to pay, you know."

"Yes, I think it's about time. What do you suggest?"

Rick was quiet for a moment, then an idea struck him.

"Let's test it. Why don't you say it's your birthday? Let's see if he gives you a nice present..."

"Perfect!" crowed Babs.

To Sixpence's consternation, the Captain's obsession with Babs didn't diminish. On the contrary, Sixpence thought it was intensifying. He watched his companion become almost hypnotised by the barmaid, and he shook his head.

"Well, Captain, you'll never guess what day it is next Wednesday," said Babs, tilting her head at him coyly and treating him to a wink.

"No, I'm sorry, Barbara, I have no idea," said the Captain.

"It's my birthday!"

"Is it? I'd like to get you a gift, what would you like?"

"Oh no, I'm not that kind of girl!" squealed Babs, and her laughter rang out.

Sixpence rolled his eyes, but neither the Captain or barmaid noticed.

"You don't have to buy little *me* a present!" she said, leaning into him and patting his knee.

The Captain's face flushed red at her touch.

"But I'd like to!"

"Well, Captain, if you must…"

That night, the Captain and Sixpence walked home in silence. The Captain, deep in thought, cleared his throat.

"Sixpence, you remember those ornaments you packed away years ago?"

"Yes, sir, I do."

"Do you remember where you stored them?"

"Of course. I wrapped them in newspaper and packed them into tea chests. They're in the cellar."

"Right! Good, good."

He said no more, but he didn't need to. The Captain was entirely devoid of any guile, and Sixpence could read him like an open book.

"Is there something you were looking for in particular?" Sixpence asked.

"Er, not exactly. I just wondered if some of that cut glass, or crystal stuff was to hand…"

"I expect I could find it without too much trouble, sir."

"Well, if you could, old man. Actually, I was thinking of that blue crystal peacock, do you remember it?"

"I do, sir. You told me it was one of your mother's favourites. Very valuable, I seem to remember."

"Ah, yes. That's the one. Could you locate it for me, please?"

"Of course, sir. May I ask what you were planning to do with it?"

The Captain's face darkened, taking on an expression that Sixpence had never seen before.

"If you *must* know, I'm planning to give it to Barbara on her birthday," he snapped.

Sixpence's jaw dropped in astonishment. Not because the Captain had admitted his plans for the crystal peacock.

No, Sixpence had already guessed that.

It was the Captain's tone of voice that astonished him. In all the years they'd been together, the Captain had never spoken to him like that.

10

"**W**hat is it?"

"Hang on! Give us a chance. Let me get it out of my bag. It's worth waiting for, honestly."

"It's all wrapped up in newspaper."

"I know, he apologised, but he said he didn't have any proper wrapping paper handy."

She peeled away the old newspaper.

"Look at this!" said Rick, holding up a scrap. "It's dated 1969 and the headline is about the Kray twins being found guilty of murder."

"1969? Well, the present he gave me is

much older than that. He said it belonged to his mother."

Babs pulled away the last piece of newspaper and the crystal peacock was revealed. Rick gasped and took it from her, turning it over in his hands.

"Wow, that's an antique. It'll be worth a pretty penny."

"I know! When he gave it to me, I says to him, I says, 'Ooooh, Captain, that's so beeeutiful!' And he says, 'Oh, I'm very pleased you like it, dear lady.' So then I gave him a big kiss on the cheek, and the poor feller nearly fainted." Babs roared with laughter at the memory.

"So what did you say next?"

"So I says, 'Ooooh, Captain, how did you know I collect these?' And he says, 'Do you? Then I'll bring you some more.' Honestly, Rick, as long as that sidekick of his, Sixpence, doesn't stick his oar in, I think we've found ourselves a golden goose!"

Easter had long passed, and clumps of faded daffodils swayed on the village green. April showers had made the grass lush and vibrant.

The cricket season had started, and weekends saw villagers dressed in white, playing the ancient game on the green. The sound of willow hitting leather, and cries of "Howzat!" followed by spontaneous little bursts of applause rang round the village.

The date of the village fête was approaching, and the committee was finalising arrangements for the weekend in June when the fête would take place on the village green.

Babs had become accepted at the pub, and Angus was delighted that his takings were on the rise. It seemed that the clientele of the Dew Drop Inn liked the brashness of the woman and enjoyed seeing her behind the bar.

However, one man eyed the barmaid suspiciously. Sixpence had watched the collection of crystal ornaments stored in the cellar diminish, one by one. Each time Babs had unwrapped another, she squealed with delight, rewarding her admirer with a kiss on the cheek, rendering him pink with pleasure.

When the crystal had gone, the Captain presented her with other ornaments: buddhas, carved animals, ornate boxes and trinkets, all precious items that his grandfather had brought back from India.

Sixpence's heart sank lower daily. His employer was no judge of character and Sixpence was quite convinced that no happiness would result from this dalliance. Babs was a coquette, but a clever one. Sixpence had witnessed her winking at other customers and flirting outrageously but only when she was sure that the Captain couldn't see her.

Something, too, had shifted in his own relationship with the Captain. No longer were they so easy in each other's company, and something unspoken lurked between them.

I've got to try and stop this, make him see sense before he gets in too deep, he thought to himself as he tended his roses. *Who is Babs Mason anyway? Where does she come from, and what is her history?*

The more he thought about it, the more he was resolved to carry out some detective work and prove that she was not a woman to be trusted.

And there were only two people who could answer his questions.

Her employer, Angus McDonald.

And Babs Mason herself.

Sixpence leaned on the bar next to Stan Cooper. He had left the Captain and Babs to their own devices in the inglenook. He stole a guilty look over his shoulder to ensure that neither was watching him. To the contrary, the pair were absorbed in each other. Babs was throwing back her head and laughing, while the Captain patted her hand fondly.

"Ah, Sixpence, can I get you anything?" asked the landlord.

"Thank you, Angus, but I don't need a

drink. I did wonder whether you could help me with a rather, um, delicate matter."

"Shall I leave?" asked Stan, stepping back. He apologised profusely as his steel-capped size ten boots crushed another customer's toe. Stan's keen detective mind hadn't cured his clumsiness.

"No, no, Stan. Please stay. It isn't a criminal matter, exactly, but I wouldn't mind your opinion."

"Fire away, old man," said Angus. "We'll do our best to help."

Angus, Stan and Sixpence put their heads together, and Sixpence took a deep breath. He shuffled from one foot to the other.

"It's like this," Sixpence began in a low voice, then plunged on. "I'm worried about the Captain."

"Why?" asked Angus.

"The Captain hasn't had much experience with women," said Sixpence carefully, "and I'm really worried that he's been taken for a ride."

Stan said nothing, but he was listening

intently. Another peal of Babs's laughter rang out behind them.

"You mean his friendship with Babs?" asked Angus.

"Yes, I'm afraid so. He's absolutely smitten by her."

"Well, there's no law against that," said Stan, smiling.

"I know!" said Sixpence hurriedly. "It's just that he's givin' her a stream of presents. Valuable antiques from the manor. Stuff that's been packed away for decades."

"No law against that, either," said Stan, but he was no longer smiling.

"It's just, I wondered whether either of you knew anything about her or her past," finished Sixpence. "I mean, you read in the papers about these professional fraudsters… Perhaps I'm completely wrong, but it just doesn't feel right. Do you know what I mean?"

Angus and Stan nodded.

"Well," said Angus quietly. "She said she's a single woman. She came with two glowing references from other pubs. Somerset area, I think. To be honest, I didn't check them out at the time, I was so busy, but I could look them up in the Yellow Pages and give them a ring. Nobody needs serving at the moment, I'll pop out the back and do it right now. I hope you're wrong about this, because she's a good barmaid!"

"I'd be really grateful," said Sixpence.

Stan said nothing, but he was deep in thought. If he turned sideways, he could see Babs quite clearly in the inglenook. Her left hand rested on the Captain's knee. He focused on the third finger. No wedding ring, but her finger was indented, the way a woman's finger becomes when she's worn a ring for years.

Was Sixpence right?

Was Babs Mason hiding some secrets?

"Hello, am I through to the White Hart?"

"Yes, you are, how can I help you?"

"I'm sorry to disturb you, but I was wondering if you could help me. My name's Angus McDonald and I'm the landlord of the Dew Drop in Sixpenny Cross, Dorset. Who am I speaking with, please?"

"My name's Sarah, I'm the landlady here. How can I help you, Mr McDonald?"

"I've recently hired a new barmaid, Babs Mason. She worked for you, and she gave me a reference signed by the landlord, David Leech."

The line went silent for several seconds. Then Sarah spoke again.

"I'm sorry, but are you sure you have the right pub? There's no David Leech here. My husband is the landlord, and his name is Daniel Falconbridge. We've had the White Hart for twelve years and I'm quite sure we've never had a barmaid here called Babs Mason."

11

*A*ngus McDonald put the telephone down, perplexed.

Good gracious!

He ran his fingers through his hair.

Was Sixpence right? If Babs was lying about her past job at the White Hart, what else was she hiding?

Sixpence had returned to the inglenook, and Babs was back behind the bar.

"Ah, there you are, Boss," she cried, "I thought you'd been whisked away by aliens!" And she threw her head back, laughing.

Stan Cooper watched her with interest,

then turned to Angus, raising his eyebrows in question.

Angus leaned in to him and whispered, "The pub in Somerset."

"Yes?"

"They've never heard of her."

Stan's brow furrowed but he wasn't very surprised.

"Don't tell her what you know yet," he instructed. "When you get the chance, phone the other pub, check out their reference too. That'll give me time to make a few enquiries of my own."

"Do you need some more time to think about it?" asked the salesman.

"No, I don't think so, do you?" Babs turned to check with her husband.

"If you can knock a bit more off the price, we'll take it," said Rick. "We'll pay cash, of course."

"Wise decision," said the salesman. "You can't go wrong with these Ford Escorts.

Very reliable cars. This one may be secondhand, but it'll go on for ever."

They agreed on a price and Rick pulled out a wad of banknotes from his pocket. He counted them out on the desk, licking his finger occasionally and placing the notes in neat one-hundred piles. Then he passed them over to the salesman to count. Satisfied, the man unlocked a drawer and put the money away before handing Rick the car's keys and logbook.

"A pleasure doing business with you," said Rick, as they left.

"Oooh, Rick! It's so nice to have a car of our own again, isn't it? I'll be able to drive myself to work now instead of taking the bus," cooed Babs as they drove away. "And I saw you watching where he keeps the money! You're not thinking of turning the place over, are you?"

Rick laughed, and patted her knee.

"Once a con, always a con," he chuckled. "I learned in prison it's always a good idea to use your eyes. You never know when you might need to know where people stash their cash."

"Thanks to the Captain, I think we have happy days ahead," laughed Babs. "It's my night off, let's raise a glass or two to our golden goose tonight, thank him for our new car."

"Good idea. And it's time we started to think about how to get you inside that manor house of his. I reckon it's packed with valuables, and I bet he wouldn't even notice if some went missing."

"I don't think he would either," agreed Babs, smiling at the thought, then sobering. "I think his companion, Sixpence, is a lot more switched on, though. We can't rush into anything."

"Hmm," said Rick thoughtfully, "it would be even better if we could get rid of our friend Sixpence altogether."

"Yes, that's right, Sixpenny Cross, near Yewbridge. Am I speaking with the landlord of the King's Arms?"

"Indeed you are, how can I help?"

"Just a quick staff question, if you don't

mind. Did you have a Babs Mason working for you at any time? Maybe she called herself Barbara?"

"Barbara? No, definitely not. My ex-wife's called Barbara, and I'd remember *that* name, no question. We've never had a Barbara, or Babs, working here."

Time marched on, and May saw the first swallows arriving from Africa. A cuckoo called from Sixpenny Woods. Angus no longer lit the fire in the Dew Drop, but the Captain and Sixpence still sat in their customary seats in the inglenook, often joined by Babs.

The month of June brought out all the wildflowers in the surrounding meadows. Garden beds burst with blooms all the colours of the rainbow.

The Captain gazed out of the drawing room window onto the wide lawns edged with herbaceous borders. In his mind's eye he saw Sixpence's father using twine and stakes to tie up and support the tall lupins, foxgloves and gladioli, preventing them from falling over in strong winds.

So many years ago!

Now a professional landscaping company tended the grounds. Except, of course, for the roses and kitchen garden which were Sixpence's pride and joy.

The place needs a woman, thought the Captain. *It's too late to fill the house with children, but at least I can keep my promise and bring home a wife.*

Yes, it was time to take action.

Meanwhile, outside, Sixpence gazed at his roses. There were several buds that he had his eye on, lavishing them with time and attention. Any of these might be the blooms he would choose on the morning of the village fête, to enter in the Best Roses competition. He smiled, confident that he'd win another red rosette. His roses never failed to lift his sagging spirits. This business between Babs and the Captain was driving him to distraction lately.

Should I talk to the Captain about my suspicions? he mused. *No. Not yet.*

Stan Cooper had asked him and Angus

to maintain silence for the moment while he investigated further.

"After all," Stan had said, when Angus had reported back about the second pub Babs had allegedly worked in, "she lied, but she hasn't actually broken the law. And she has no criminal record that I can find. But mark my words, people like her may be very clever, but they always make a mistake. For the moment, we just watch and wait."

Angus was only happy to agree. Babs was an excellent barmaid and attracting an ever increasing clientele. The pub was thriving and, despite her lies, he was reluctant to fire her.

But it was hard for Sixpence to see the Captain fall ever more deeply under Babs's spell. The man was mesmerised by her, oblivious to her lack of breeding and her brassiness. The thought that the Captain might be considering making the wretched woman the lady of the manor made him shudder.

"Sixpence, is that you?" called the Captain from the drawing room, when

Sixpence entered the kitchen through the back door.

"Yes, sir."

"Can I have a quick word?"

"Of course, sir."

Sixpence entered the drawing room and waited.

"Ah, there you are, old man. I've been thinking I'd like to hold a dinner party some time, would you have any objection?"

The Captain's tone was light but Sixpence was astute enough to detect a hint of uncertainty in his employer's voice, as though he was nervous of Sixpence's reaction.

"No, of course not, sir. How many guests?"

"Oh, just one, I think."

Sixpence's heart sank. He didn't need a planetary-sized brain to guess the identity of the proposed guest.

"May I ask who?"

"Of course, I was thinking of asking Barbara from the pub. She said to me only the other day that she'd love to see

Sixpenny Manor and that she really enjoys looking at antique furniture."

I bet she does, thought Sixpence, but managed to keep his features impassive.

"Nothing too fancy," continued the Captain. "Just a nice homemade soup perhaps, and maybe roast chicken to follow. She's a simple creature."

Simple? That woman is more cunning than a starving fox.

"Perhaps, if you wouldn't mind, you could unpack a couple of the silver candlesticks, and cut a few roses for the vases?"

"Very good, sir. When were you thinking of holding this little, um, soirée?"

"I thought Thursday next week. That's Barbara's next evening off. Would that suit?"

"Indeed, sir."

"Sixpence, perhaps I shouldn't ask, but I get the impression that you don't like Barbara very much. Am I right?"

12

Sixpence opened his mouth. Here was his opportunity. The Captain had asked him a direct question. He could answer with the truth.

That woman is a lying fraud. In my opinion, she's after your money.

That was what he wanted to say, but he held his tongue.

"Sixpence?"

"It's not for me to say, sir."

"Very well. If you have any reservations, I'm sure you'll let me know in your own good time."

"Yes, sir."

"He's invited me to dinner at the manor house next Thursday," crowed Babs.

"Oh, lah-de-dah!"

"Yeah, I'll have to get myself a little black dress!"

"Never mind that, you just make sure you take a good look round. Case the joint, memorise the layout. See which rooms have good stuff in them."

"I will, don't worry. Have I ever let you down?"

"Nope, we're a great team. I just wish we could get rid of the golden goose's mate, he's the only fly in the ointment."

"You'll think of something, Rick, you always do."

It was five o'clock when the telephone on the counter rang. Stan reached for the receiver but his elbow caught his mug of tea, sending it spinning before it smashed in two on the floor. Tea splattered over the counter, threatening a pile of paperwork, and a growing, brown puddle collected at his feet.

He rolled his eyes in annoyance but grabbed the receiver just before the telephone stopped ringing.

"Sixpenny Cross Police Station, PC Cooper speaking."

"Ah Stan, thought I'd missed you. It's PC Holman here at Yewbridge cop shop. Thought I'd give you a quick bell."

"How are you?" asked Stan, watching with dismay as his papers began to soak up the spilled tea.

"Fine, thank you. You wanted us to check out a Barbara Mason, I think, a few weeks ago?"

Stan forgot about the tea.

"Yes, that's right. You couldn't find anything on her. She had no rap sheet."

"That's true, but we've just come across something else. I thought it might be worth telling you."

Stan waited, unaware he was now standing in a pool of tea.

"Barbara Mason kept her maiden name,

but she's actually married to Richard Kane. And he's got a rap sheet as long as your arm."

"Really? What for?"

"Just about everything. He's a nasty piece of work. Burglary, car theft, fraud, grievous bodily harm, you name it. He's had a few stretches inside. He was also the main suspect for a homicide back in the seventies, but the case was dropped through lack of evidence. It was a bungled burglary. The homeowner surprised the burglars so they clobbered him over the head with a crowbar. He died of a heart attack."

"And Babs Mason is married to this thug?"

"Yup, looks like it. They live together in a council flat in Yewbridge."

"Well, thank you. You've been most helpful."

Stan stood still for several minutes, deep in thought. It was time to have a word with the Captain. Better still, he'd first have a chat with Sixpence and together they'd work out the best way to break the unwelcome news to the Captain.

Yes, he decided. *I'll catch Sixpence at the pub tonight and bend his ear.*

Decision made, he locked up and went home, unaware of the great, wet footprints he left criss-crossing the floor.

But PC Stan Cooper didn't see Sixpence that evening. It was Thursday and neither the Captain nor Sixpence were at the pub. They were entertaining Babs at the manor house.

The Captain had taken extra care with his appearance. His sparse hair was slicked down with water, and his fingernails were spotless. He wore a crisp white shirt and cravat, feeling they were in keeping with the occasion.

What exactly was the occasion? he asked himself.

He had no precise answer to this question but planned to see how the evening went. For some reason he felt that something huge was about to happen.

Sixpence, in spite of his misgivings, had worked hard. He had uncovered the dining room table and chairs and polished the wood until it gleamed. White candles flickered in silver candlesticks, and he'd arranged some of his roses in vases. The table was set perfectly and the silverware sparkled.

"You'll dine with us, of course, old man?" the Captain had asked, but Sixpence had politely refused.

"No, sir, I'll leave you two in peace. It'll leave me free to serve, too."

The truth was, he didn't think he could stomach watching Babs fawn all over the Captain. He didn't want to listen to her peals of fake laughter while the Captain gazed at her as though she was Miss World 1985.

Babs had swept up the gravel drive in her new Ford Escort, and the Captain had welcomed her. She was wearing a tight black dress that hugged her ample curves. A necklace drew the eye to her décolletage, and her scarlet lips pouted. She tilted her head, allowing him to kiss her cheek, and he walked her through to the drawing room.

"Can I get you a drink, Barbara?" he asked. "Perhaps a sherry?"

"Oooh! Perhaps a sweet sherry, thank you! Just a little one, mind, don't want you getting me tipsy!"

A peal of empty laughter rang out, and, in the kitchen, Sixpence grimaced and rolled his eyes.

The Captain stuck his head round the kitchen door.

"Sixpence, I'm just going to show Barbara round the house, we shouldn't be long."

"Very good, sir, I'll have the first course waiting for you when you get back."

As he stirred the homemade vegetable soup, he could hear her laughter reverberating from different parts of the house. Many of the rooms were closed, but she seemed to want to see them all.

When the pair had returned and seated themselves at the dining room table, Sixpence served the soup, ensuring each bowl had a sprig of watercress garnish and a final dash of cream.

"Thank you, Sixpence, that looks very good," said the Captain.

"Look what the Captain just gave me," said Babs, showing Sixpence the exquisitely carved ivory elephant that usually sat on the hall table next to the telephone.

Sixpence said nothing.

"My grandfather brought that back from India a hundred years ago. It has a raised trunk which is supposed to be lucky," said the Captain. "It was much prized by my mother. She always said that if it stood facing the front door, it would protect all who live here. I'm glad you like it."

"I'll put it here, out of your way," said Sixpence, moving it to the sideboard before returning to the kitchen.

When they had finished, Sixpence cleared away the empty soup plates.

"Excellent soup," said the Captain. "It's a pity you can't enter it in the fête this weekend, I'm sure it would win a prize."

"Thank you, sir," said Sixpence and brought in the next course.

The fragrant roast chicken steamed as he

served it. He was lifting off the lids to the fresh vegetables when the telephone rang.

"Who can that be? You get it, Sixpence," said the Captain, "we can manage."

Sixpence hurried to the telephone in the hall, trying to ignore Babs's voice behind him.

"Let me serve you, Captain. You just tell me when to stop…" and her laughter rang out.

The hall table looked strange and empty without the ivory elephant.

"Sixpenny Manor," he said into the telephone receiver. "Who's calling?"

"Sixpence, is that you?"

13

"Sixpence speakin', who am I talkin' with?"

"Sixpence, it's me," said the voice, "Stan Cooper. Can you talk or might you be overheard?"

"It's not a good time," Sixpence said quietly.

"Right, answer yes or no. I'm guessing the Captain and Babs Mason are within earshot?"

"Yes."

"Listen carefully. I found out something rather disturbing today. I was going to tell you at the pub but Angus just told me that you and the Captain were holding a dinner party for Babs tonight. It's just possible that you and the Captain may be in some danger. Babs Mason is married to a villain."

Sixpence gasped and found himself glancing over his shoulder.

"She's married to an old con with a record as long as your arm. He's a thief, but that's not all, he's violent. I'm guessing that he's sent her to case the manor. Has she walked round the house?"

"Yes."

"As I thought."

"What shall I do?" whispered Sixpence.

"Nothing. Don't do anything yet, leave it with me. I don't think you have anything to fear from her, it's what her husband is planning that worries me. Make sure you lock all your doors and windows tonight, and stay on the alert."

When Sixpence replaced the receiver, his hand was shaking.

I knew it! he whispered to himself. *I just knew it!*

He stood for a moment, digesting this latest news, then entered the dining room.

"Ah, there you are, old man," said the

Captain. "Who was it? Anything important?"

Always the gentleman, the Captain had been doing his best to be as pleasant as possible, aware that Babs and Sixpence were wary of each other.

"No, no. Just my old mother calling from Worthing. I'll phone her back another time for a proper chat. How's the roast chicken?"

"Delicious, old boy! You surpassed yourself. Barbara is really enjoying it, too. Aren't you, my dear?"

Babs nodded as she chewed.

"I'm a good cook, too, Captain. You'll have to let *me* cook for you one day," she said, her mouth still full.

"Nothing would give me more pleasure, my dear," said the Captain gazing at her fondly, and his tone spoke volumes.

Sixpence retreated to the kitchen as fast as etiquette would allow.

The evening dragged on.

Sixpence served the dessert, followed by coffee and liqueurs in the drawing room. Then he tidied the kitchen, waiting impatiently for the evening to end.

At last he heard the Captain call.

"Sixpence, Barbara is leaving. She'd like to thank you."

"I bet," he growled, but joined them on the gravel driveway.

Although it was after ten o'clock, it was still quite light, as is the norm during British summers. Babs was already sitting in her car with the window wound down and the engine running.

"Thank you for the meal, Sixpence," she called.

"Don't mention it."

The Captain patted her hand which was resting on the steering wheel, then leaned down through the window to peck her on the cheek.

Suddenly, her hand flew to her mouth in alarm.

"My elephant! I forgot my elephant!"

"Don't you worry, my dear," said the Captain, swinging round. "I'll get it for you in a trice. I know exactly where it is."

He hurried past Sixpence and into the house, intent on his act of chivalry.

Babs looked up at Sixpence and her eyes widened a little.

"Who are you staring at?" she asked.

The rage that Sixpence had been trying so hard to keep in check was threatening to bubble over.

"You, actually."

He stepped forward then leaned down into the car, bringing his face close to hers.

"What … what do you …?" she stammered.

"I know who you are, Barbara Mason, and I know what you're tryin' to do. If you, or that villain you're married to, harm a hair on the Captain's head, I swear, I'll…"

But he never finished his sentence.

Babs's foot stamped on the accelerator pedal and the car shot away, showering him with gravel and leaving gouges in the driveway.

Sixpence turned to see the Captain standing on the doorstep, white-faced, frozen in astonishment, the elephant still clutched in his hand. He ran over to his employer and, taking him by the arm, guided him back into the house.

"What happened?" asked the Captain. "Why didn't she wait for me?"

"Captain, I think we need to talk..."

"Wait! It was something you said, wasn't it? You chased her off!"

"No! Sir, that woman isn't right for you. Please listen, I'll explain!"

"That woman? Did you just call Barbara *that woman?*" The Captain held onto the mantlepiece for support. His complexion had turned from white to red.

"Sir, I..."

"I was planning to ask *that woman* to marry me," spat the Captain. "I think you guessed that and you're jealous, aren't you? You don't want her to join us here, do you? I don't know what you said to her, but I can tell you this, Peter Anderson, my debt to you ends now."

Sixpence gaped, but the Captain hadn't finished. His eyes narrowed to slits as he hissed his next words.

"You may have saved my life back in London all those years ago, but I've repaid you. Remember, I pulled you out of the gutter. I employed you. I gave you a roof over your head. I shared my home with you. Now I intend to ask *that woman* to be my wife."

"Captain!"

"But you can't let that happen, can you?"

"No! Captain! Babs isn't who you think she is! I beg you, please listen…"

"You ungrateful, scheming wretch! I will *not* listen to you," he said through clenched teeth, his lips bloodless with fury.

He slammed the elephant down on the mantlepiece and folded his arms.

"Listen to me carefully, Peter Anderson, I intend to give Barbara this elephant tomorrow, and I'm planning to ask for her hand in marriage."

"I'm sorry, Captain," said Sixpence gently, "but I don't think that's possible."

He hoped that his tone might calm the Captain, make him listen to reason and return him to his senses. Unfortunately, it had the opposite effect.

"Do you intend to stop me?" asked the Captain, barely able to contain his rage.

"Not me, Captain, but the law. I believe that Babs is already married."

"Now you've gone too far. I think it's better if you go. I want you to leave Sixpenny Manor," he said, his eyes glittering. "Pack your things and go. I never want to lay eyes on you again."

"You must listen to me, Captain! Babs Mason cannot be trusted! She's playin' you for a fool…"

"Get out!" the Captain shouted. "Get out!"

"Captain…"

But the Captain was bereft of all reason.

"Get out!" he screamed.

14

It was Friday evening and the Dew Drop Inn was buzzing.

"On your own tonight?" asked Angus when the Captain entered the pub. "No Sixpence?"

"No," said the Captain shortly, then took a breath. "Sixpence has left Sixpenny Cross."

"Oh, really? Problems with his mother in Worthing?"

The Captain didn't reply. His eyes were downcast and his face was expressionless.

Jayne Fairweather had overheard the exchange.

"Captain," she said, "the entries are

closed now for the produce and flower competitions for the fête on Sunday. Did I hear you say Sixpence has gone away?"

"Yes, that's right."

"That's good news!" chipped in Archie Draper, always the comedian. "Now my Emily has a chance of winning this year's rose competition."

Everybody laughed, except Babs, who stood behind the bar, listening and watching intently. Without looking up, the Captain made his way to the inglenook and sat down. Only then did he raise his head to search for Babs. His eyes lit up when he spotted her behind the bar. Babs treated him to a wink and a little wave of her hand. The Captain blushed.

PC Stan Cooper stood in the shadows, watching. He saw Babs pull back the handle of the pump, allowing beer to rush into the pint glass she held.

"Mind your backs," she called, pushing through the crowd to reach the Captain.

"There you go, Captain. How are you today?"

"I brought you your elephant," he said

awkwardly, relishing her nearness as she leaned down to place the pint in front of him.

"Oh, you darling man!" she said, putting her hand on his arm and enjoying seeing him blush. "You shouldn't have!"

The Captain put the elephant down and reached for her hand.

"Barbara, I'm so sorry about last night. I don't know what Sixpence said to you, but he had no right, no right at all."

"Well, I don't think he's ever liked me..."

"I told him that I didn't intend to give you up."

"Oh!"

"He's gone now, and won't trouble you again. And I hope you will continue to spend time with me."

"Of course I will, silly, it'll be my pleasure."

The Captain beamed, then looked more serious. "Barbara, I need to talk to you about ... about matters close to my heart..."

"Babs! Customers!" called Angus, and Babs turned away.

"We'll talk later," she said, with a wink. "Don't want to lose my job!"

"If you'll be mine, my dear, you'll never need to work again," he said under his breath, as Babs walked away.

The bar was particularly busy that evening, as the fête committee had just had their final meeting.

"Weather forecast looks okay for the weekend," commented Daisy Grainger, "thank goodness."

"We've been lucky most years," said Jayne Fairweather. "The marquee company will be here tomorrow to put the marquee up, and, fingers crossed, I think everything is pretty much in place."

"Yes, I'll get the tractor out and give the green a final mow in the morning before they come," said Archie. "The vicar has done a good job of pulling it all together, as usual. Barring an act of God, it should all be smooth sailing on Sunday. But then we *do* have the vicar on our side," he added, and everybody laughed.

Talk of past fêtes, interspersed with cries of, "Who's for another drink?" filled the pub, and Babs was spared only a few minutes to chat with her admirer. Realising he was unlikely to enjoy much private time with her that evening, the Captain left early.

"I'll see you tomorrow," said Babs, and squeezed his hand.

"Yes, yes! Good night, my dear. I shall look forward to it."

Stan Cooper remained in the shadows, one hand in his pocket, fiddling with the books of raffle tickets that Jayne had handed him earlier. He waited for a lull, then approached the bar.

"Excuse me, Babs," he said lightly. "Totally out of interest, you know. I wondered if you knew where Sixpence had gone."

Babs jumped, reddening.

"How should I know?"

"Weren't you having dinner at Sixpenny Manor last night?"

"Yes, but…"

"Well, did Sixpence say anything about leaving the village?"

"Not to me, he didn't."

"So you don't know where he went?"

"No, why should I? But he did get a phone call from his old mother in Worthing though."

"Did he, indeed. Thank you for that information."

Babs backed away, but Stan beckoned her forward again.

"Just one more thing," he said quietly. "Not many people know who you really are, Babs. But I do. And now that Sixpence has gone, the whole village will be looking out for the Captain. He's very well liked here."

Babs's eyes widened.

"Oh, and Babs, give my regards to Rick."

***

Jayne Fairweather eyed the skies on Saturday morning as she opened the post office and general store. All clear, she decided, and therefore a good day to prepare for the village fête the next day. Archie Draper waved as he rumbled his tractor onto the green, the attachment he towed already scything through the lush summer grass. Jayne sniffed. She loved the smell of newly mown grass.

A steady stream of customers kept her busy that morning, but she noted the arrival of a truck with *Marilla's Marquees* emblazoned on the side. The village always used the same company. Six men jumped out and, after consulting a map, identified where the marquee should be set up on the far side of the green.

When Jayne next looked, she saw the men marking out the site, driving pegs into the ground. Even at this distance, the rhythmic hammering filled the air.

Suddenly, a man shouted. The banging stopped and, to her amazement, the men flung down their tools and ran as though chased by bulls. The first two burst through the shop doorway.

"Quick, phone the police! We've come across an unexploded bomb!"

Jayne didn't need telling twice and grabbed the telephone.

"Stan? Jayne here. I'm with the marquee people. They've found an unexploded bomb on the green."

Following a short conversation, Jayne put down the receiver and looked up. The men had crowded into the shop, waiting for her to speak.

"PC Cooper is alerting the bomb disposal unit now," she said. He's on his way but he's asked if we can make sure nobody goes near the area. Unfortunately this isn't the first time unexploded shells have been found around here."

The men nodded and went outside. They stood in a huddle for a moment then fanned out, keeping a healthy distance from where they had been working.

Jayne snatched up the receiver again and dialled the rectory's number.

"Vicar? Jayne here. We've got a bit of a crisis. The marquee men found an unexploded bomb on the village green."

"Good heavens! Has Stan been told?"

"Yes, he's informed the bomb disposal squad. Everything is under control. But the big problem is, I doubt we'll be able to use the green for the fête!"

"Oh my goodness. You're right, by the

time they diffuse the bomb there'll be no time to put the marquee up."

"And the bomb people will want to scour the whole green in case there are more."

"Yes, yes," the vicar thought for a moment. "Well, we can't move it here, the rectory gardens are just too small. There's only one other place really."

"Sixpenny Manor?"

"Exactly."

"Do you think the Captain will agree?"

"I think so. I'll reassure him, tell him that nobody will disturb him or invade his privacy. We only need the gardens and I'll promise him that the committee will make sure everything is as we found it when we leave."

Saturday had been a rough day for the Captain. The visit from the vicar had turned his world upside down. As if he didn't have enough on his mind, with Babs and Sixpence, now he was being asked to allow the general public into the grounds of the manor house.

"We'll put *No Entry* signs up," the vicar had said. "The public will only be allowed on the lawn, not the walled garden, and definitely not in the house. Just keep all the doors locked, Captain, and nobody will bother you."

The Captain knew that his parents would have agreed immediately, as would Sixpence, had he been there, so he reluctantly relented. A simple man, he found it difficult to cope with any changes to his routine, Lately, there had been just too many.

From the drawing room window he saw the marquee go up. Then Archie Draper arrived on his tractor, pulling a trailer heaped with trestle tables and chairs. Simon Grainger helped him unload and the pair carried the tables into the marquee to set up. In and out, in and out, like bees in a hive.

It was enough to make a man dizzy.

Members of the committee kept arriving

all afternoon, bringing items like blackboards and stacks of white tablecloths.

But the Captain's mind was only partially diverted. Most of his thoughts were centred on one person: his passion, his hope for the future.

Barbara.

The pub will be busy again tonight, he mused, *and I doubt I'll be able to get Barbara on her own. I'll just pop in for a quick pint. But when the fête is over, then I'll ask her if she'll be mine. Nothing will stand in my way.*

The thought made him tremble almost uncontrollably but also warmed him from the top of his head to the tips of his toes.

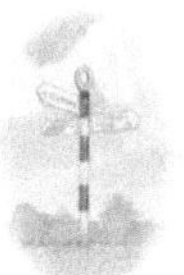

15

At the pub that night, conversation centred around the discovery of the unexploded shell. Dorset had been a major target during the second world war and, years later, the discovery of unexploded bombs was a common occurrence.

The bomb disposal unit arrived from nearby Bovington. They removed the bomb and then conducted a thorough search of the village green. All the cottages skirting the village green, including the pub and post office, were evacuated. Many hours later, the area was declared safe and everyone was allowed back.

When the Captain entered the pub, a cheer went up.

"Pour that man a drink!" shouted Archie Draper. "If it wasn't for him, the fête wouldn't be going ahead tomorrow."

Hands clapped the Captain's back.

"No, no," he protested, awkward as always, "it's nothing."

The Captain was too socially inept to interact easily with the villagers, even though he had known most of them all his life. The attention was too much for him, and he soon left, having only enjoyed the briefest of glimpses of his love behind the bar.

Never mind, he told himself, *I must be patient. Soon Barbara and I will be together for ever.*

Early the next morning, the stall-holders began to arrive, and the Captain observed the activity from the drawing room window. True to his word, the vicar arrived and hung *No Entry,* and *Private* notices on all the manor house doors, and on the gate into the walled garden.

On the outer lawns, a coconut shy was erected, as well as a skittle alley and a hoopla stall. Cloths were flung over tables, and posters and placards fixed up proclaiming "Guess the weight of the cake" and "How many sweets in the jar?" A tombola appeared, and also a 'Test your strength' machine.

A long, thick rope was laid on the ground in readiness for the tug-of-war, and vans began to arrive that would serve burgers, popcorn and candyfloss. An inflatable bouncy castle began to pulse and raise itself from the ground as air was pumped into it.

Unseen, the Captain watched it all.

Blast it, Sixpence! he couldn't help thinking. *You would have enjoyed all this!*

But then he remembered Barbara, and the way her soft hand felt in his.

Villagers began arriving carrying cake tins, jam and pickle jars, vegetables, fruit, flowers and all manner of produce. They disappeared into the marquee to set up their entries on the tables, ready for judging.

Somebody else would win the *Best Rose* competition this year, while Sixpence's prize roses would be left to wilt and rot unseen within the walled garden.

Suddenly, the Captain felt an overwhelming urge to see his lady love.

He looked at his watch. It was one o'clock and the pub would remain open until two. Plenty of time. He could walk down to the Dew Drop and order himself a Ploughman's Lunch from the menu. A good slice of thick, crusty bread with cheese and pickle and a salad garnish would make a nice change for lunch. And he could feast his eyes on Barbara, even if she was busy.

He couldn't remember the last time he had visited the Dew Drop at lunchtime. The thought of surprising Barbara put a little spring in his step and his heart raced faster as he locked the house and headed towards the pub.

He didn't hear the telephone in the hall ringing.

PC Stan Cooper was uneasy. The Captain wasn't answering his telephone.

"He's probably in the grounds, watching the preparations for the fête," his wife, Sally, said. "I wouldn't worry."

"Yes, I'm sure that's what it is. I'm going to walk over there soon anyway, those raffle tickets won't sell themselves."

He and Sally had been discussing the Captain's obvious passion for Babs. Both had agreed that, although the Dew Drop's barmaid hadn't broken any laws, it was probably wise to tell the Captain what they had discovered about her.

"It's for his own protection," said Sally.

"I don't think he'll take it very well," said Stan, shaking his head. "He's not really a man of the world."

"I think you *have* to warn him," said Sally. "Imagine if the manor house was broken into, or worse, and you'd known about her and her husband all the time. You'd never forgive yourself!"

"No, you're right. I must have a chat with him, man to man, and sooner rather than later."

Outside the Dew Drop Inn, wide red parasols advertising beers shaded wooden tables. People were seated enjoying cold drinks and pub snacks.

Even before the Captain entered the pub, he heard laughter ringing out through the door that had been flung open to let in the summer breezes. He smiled, recognising her voice mingling with others.

Always the life and soul of the party, he thought fondly. *So unlike me! Whatever does she see in me?*

He stepped into the pub and stood still, scanning the interior, his eyes adjusting to the dark, eager to see her. The hilarity he had heard emanated from one particular table.

And Babs was at the centre of it.

Three men sat round the table, drinking and laughing. A fourth man had Babs perched on his knee, her back to the Captain. The man's arm encircled her waist.

The Captain froze.

"Go on," the man begged, "one more kiss and I'll buy you another drink."

"Just one, then," Babs exclaimed and landed a long kiss on the man's waiting lips. "There you go!" she shrieked, and threw back her head, filling the pub with peals of laughter.

The men were all cheering and raising their glasses, but the Captain had seen enough. He turned and blundered out of the pub, past the outside tables, in the direction of the manor house.

Images flashed through his head, so vivid that they almost blinded him, making him stumble as he headed home.

Barbara.

Barbara flirting with men.

Barbara kissing another man.

Margaret.

Margaret in Kensington Gardens.

Margaret telling him she had met somebody else.

His dying father.

His promise to his father.
And finally, Sixpence.

16

  Blind to everybody and everything, the Captain staggered home and pushed the key into the lock. He turned it and entered the coolness, shutting out the sounds of the fête. Leaning his back against the door, he felt more protected from the outside world, but waves of nausea swept over him and he found breathing difficult.

Gathering his strength, he lurched to the kitchen, drew the bolt and opened the door to the walled garden.

The fête was in full swing. Madonna's latest song, *Crazy for You,* blared from a loudspeaker. Children screamed as they bounced on the inflatable castle, and adults called each other.

"Hold tight!" yelled parents to their youngsters as they trotted past on Shetland pony rides.

"Sorry, missed! Have another go," urged stall holders when punters lost their money attempting to hook ducks or throw hoops over targets.

But the Captain heard nothing.

He stumbled past the neat rows of vegetables that Sixpence had grown from seed. Lettuce, spinach and clambering broad beans, all ready for picking. As he passed the herb bed, one shoe brushed the pungent mint plants, but he smelled nothing.

A spade leaned against the wall, soil still clinging to it.

Panting, he finally reached his destination.

The rose garden.

On an ordinary day, the Captain would have enjoyed and admired the blooms. Perfect buds, poised, and others already open, showing the sun their velvet petals and exquisite colours.

The Captain stepped off the path and into the bushes, paying no heed to the cruel thorns that scratched his skin.

He stood, tears coursing down his cheeks, aware of a growing pressure and tightening of his chest.

"Sixpence!" he mouthed. "What have I done?"

Stan Cooper had already completed one circuit of the fête, selling raffle tickets. Having forgotten to bring a box, he stored the bought tickets in his upturned police helmet, much to everybody's amusement. It was a good plan, except that sometimes the breeze sent the tickets hurtling across the grass.

"I'm going to try and have a word with the Captain," he told his wife, handing her the helmet and unsold books of raffle tickets. "I shouldn't be long."

"Good luck," said Sally, "and see if you can borrow a box or something. We can't be chasing raffle tickets across the lawn all afternoon."

"Ah, a box! I'll use that as my excuse."

Aware that the Captain was unlikely to answer a knock on the front door, Stan headed for the gate to the walled garden. He ignored the large *Private, No Entry* sign and tried the handle. It was unlocked. He quietly let himself in and walked up the path to the kitchen door. Despite it being slightly ajar, he rapped it lightly with his knuckles.

No answer.

He stuck his head round the door and glanced into the empty kitchen.

"Captain? Are you there?"

No reply.

"Captain? PC Stan Cooper here. Sorry to bother you, but I wondered if you had a box or something I could borrow."

Nothing.

"For the raffle tickets…"

He listened carefully, but nothing stirred in the house. Stan pushed the door open and entered, all his senses alert.

"Captain?"

He checked the dining room, but that was empty, too.

"Captain, are you there?" he called as he entered the drawing room.

The heavy velvet curtains were drawn, shutting out the sunlight and deadening the sounds of the fête. It took a moment for his eyes to adjust to the darkness.

Stan's finger flicked the light switch, flooding the room with artificial light.

"Ah, there you are, Captain," he said, seeing the figure in the armchair. "Sorry to disturb you, but I was…"

He never finished the sentence.

Neither did the Captain answer.

The Captain's eyes were wide open, staring ahead at a spot above the mantlepiece. His hands, already cold, were clenched in his lap.

The Captain was dead.

The ambulance had to come from Yewbridge, so Stan had plenty of time to look around while he waited for it to arrive.

He was sure the Captain had died of natural causes, but he knew better than to tamper with anything. His keen eyes and sharp detective brain missed nothing.

Without touching them, he examined the Captain's clenched fists. His eyes scanned the room, absorbing every detail. He walked back out into the walled garden and prowled around. Before long, he believed he knew exactly what had happened, and was filled with sorrow.

The ambulance swept up the gravel drive, and the attendants ran up the steps.

"There's no hurry," said Stan. "I'm afraid he's already passed away."

They checked for a pulse, but there was no sign of life.

"Looks like he's had a heart attack," commented one of the attendants, "but the doctors at the hospital will confirm that."

Stan nodded.

The blue flashing light and siren had attracted the attention of the crowds at the fête, and news of the Captain's death spread like wildfire. As the body was carried down the steps on a gurney, the onlookers fell silent.

"I saw the Captain go into the Dew Drop Inn at lunchtime," somebody said in a low voice.

Stan heard the comment, and felt he probably now held the last jagged piece of the jigsaw puzzle.

When the ambulance pulled away, and the crowds had dispersed, Stan entered the house again and, with a heavy heart, contacted Yewbridge police station.

"Hello, PC Stan Cooper of Sixpenny Cross here. I wish to report a murder."

17

*A*ngus McDonald, Stan Cooper and his wife, Sally, sat around the kitchen table at the police house.

"What I'm telling you now must go no further," said Stan. "It'll all come out in the open soon enough, but I thought you'd probably need to know, Angus, as you've been in on it from the beginning."

"Of course, but I don't understand anything," said Angus, bewildered. "You say there's been a murder, but I thought the Captain died of a heart attack?"

"Yes, that's right."

"The Captain wasn't murdered, was he?"

"No."

"Then who was?"

"I'm coming to that."

"I take it my barmaid has something to do with all this, am I right?"

"Yes. I don't believe it would have happened if it hadn't been for Babs and her villainous husband. But no, I don't think they murdered anybody."

Sally frowned but said nothing, knowing that her husband would explain all in good time.

Stan took a gulp of tea from his mug.

"Sixpence told me long ago about the Captain's promise to his dying father to bring back a wife to Sixpenny Manor. But we all know that the Captain had no idea about women."

"Or anything really," remarked Sally.

"He was like putty in Babs's hands," agreed Angus. "I never liked her, but she's a jolly good barmaid."

"Exactly. The Captain fell for her, hook, line and sinker. As you know, Sixpence was very protective of the Captain. He'd saved the Captain's life once before, long ago, and

I think Sixpence felt kind of responsible for him ever since."

"They were genuinely fond of each other," said Sally. "And we all know the Captain was not exactly worldly wise."

"I think the murder occurred last Thursday, the night of the dinner party," said Stan. "I phoned Sixpence that night because I had just found out about Babs and her husband's background. I was worried that they might target the manor house, and that Babs was casing the joint. I told him not to tell the Captain yet, but I think he did. And it was too much for the Captain, which is why I think the Captain killed Sixpence."

"What?"

"The Captain killed Sixpence?"

"Yes, I believe he couldn't accept that Babs wasn't genuine. Maybe Sixpence even told him he suspected Babs was already married. The idea drove him completely insane."

"So Sixpence never went away? Have you found Sixpence's body?"

"No. But I'm pretty sure I know where it is. And I know how he was killed."

"Where?"

"How?"

"Let me explain. During the time before the ambulance arrived, I had a chance to have a good look around, and I found several things that told the story."

"Like what?"

"I looked round the walls, and there were lots of slightly darker squares and rectangles where pictures used to hang long ago. The wallpaper had faded less behind the pictures. But in one place, right above the mantlepiece, there was another, similar, much darker mark on the wall, as if something used to hang there, but had recently been removed."

"A picture?"

"No, a curved shape. I think an Indian scimitar used to hang there. A souvenir brought back by the Captain's grandfather."

Sally and Angus stared at Stan, who continued.

"In death, the Captain's eyes were open, staring at that point on the wall."

Both listeners gasped.

"I looked at the carpet. It's one of those brown, ornate Persian affairs, and there was a big stain on it. I took my handkerchief out of my pocket, moistened it with water, and rubbed at a corner of the stain. I'm positive it's blood."

Stan drew out a white handkerchief and showed them.

"It does look like blood," agreed Sally.

"Also, his hands were clenched tightly in his lap. I could see he was holding something and at first I thought it was scraps of white paper. But it wasn't."

"What was it?" breathed Sally.

"Rose petals. White rose petals. It was almost as if he was trying to confess, trying to tell us something. His expression in death showed such pain and sorrow..."

Stan stopped. The memory was a sad one. Then he took a deep breath and continued.

"The rose petals led me outside, and I found an area in the walled garden, next to Sixpenny's rose bushes. It had been cleared and well dug over recently."

"Didn't Sixpence say he was planning to cultivate chrysanthemums? Perhaps that's the spot he had chosen?"

"Yes, I think that's it. But I think that's where they will find poor Sixpence's body, and the scimitar, probably. I think the Captain killed Sixpence in a moment of blind rage, then carried him to the walled garden and buried him. It's very sad. I believe he caught sight of Babs flirting in the pub at lunchtime, and he realised he'd made a terrible mistake."

"He realised that Sixpence was telling the truth?"

"Exactly. And the shock of his dreadful mistake, and grief for Sixpence, brought on a massive heart attack."

18

Of course, when the police investigated, little one, they found everything just as Stan said they would. Poor Sixpence's body was buried in the patch where he had planned to grow prize chrysanthemums. With him was the Indian scimitar that killed him.

Stan Cooper had a fine policeman's mind, no question about that.

People still talk in whispers about the village fête of 1985. First it was almost cancelled because of the unexploded shell, then two bodies were found at the manor. As you can imagine, Sixpenny Cross made national news that month.

Babs and her husband, Richard Kane, left Yewbridge. Some say they went up north but nobody missed them, except perhaps Angus who had to advertise for a new barmaid. As Stan always said, the couple hadn't committed murder or broken any law. Even so, everyone felt that the whole sorry affair was Babs's fault. It was her greed that made her act the way she did, and caused the Captain to become unhinged.

Angus McDonald put the box of dominoes away in a dark cupboard. He always told my friend Jayne that he couldn't bear to see anybody else play with them.

Lots of people still believe that Sixpenny Manor is haunted by the ghosts of the Captain and Sixpence. I don't know about that, little one, but I do know that nothing ever grows in that spot where Sixpence was once buried, except roses. No vegetables, no chrysanthemums, no weeds, nothing.

Only roses would grow, and the white ones grew best of all.

At first, no living relatives could be found to inherit Sixpenny Manor, but the

Captain's lawyers eventually managed to track down a distant cousin.

Next time I watch over you, little one, I'm going to tell you the story of young Dexter. What a remarkable tale that is! It's remarkable because Dexter surprised everyone, including himself.

Yes, D is for Dexter, but that story is for another day.

SIXPENCE'S CREAMY SUMMER VEGETABLE SOUP

"Excellent soup," said the Captain. "It's a pity you can't enter it in the fete this weekend, I'm sure it would win a prize."

INGREDIENTS

- 1 cup sweetcorn kernels
- 1 cup green beans, sliced
- 1 cup peas
- 1 cup chopped carrot
- 4 cups vegetable stock or broth
- 2 medium potatoes, cubed

- 3 stalks celery, chopped
- 1 large onion, chopped
- 4 tbs butter
- 1 tbs garlic powder
- 3 tbs lemon juice
- Cream, sour cream or Greek-style yoghurt for serving
- Parsley or watercress for garnish

METHOD

Melt the butter in a large pot over medium-high heat.
Sauté the onion and celery for 2 minutes.
Add spices.
Continue cooking, stirring frequently for a further 2 minutes.
Add the stock and remaining vegetables. Bring to the boil.
Reduce heat to medium-low. Cover and simmer 30 minutes, or until the carrots, potato and celery are cooked.
Sieve or blend the soup until it has reached your desired consistency.

Return the soup to the stock pot. Mix well
and reheat if necessary.
Stir in the lemon juice.
Serve with a dollop of cream, sour cream or
natural Greek yogurt on top.
Garnish with parsley or a sprig of
watercress.

A REQUEST...

We authors absolutely rely on our readers' reviews. We love them even more than a glass of chilled wine on a summer's night beneath the stars.

Even more than chocolate.

If you enjoyed this book, I'd be so grateful if you left a review, even if it's simply one sentence. It's the very best way for authors to get their books noticed.

THANK YOU!

PREVIEW OF CHICKENS, MULES AND TWO OLD FOOLS

BY VICTORIA TWEAD

If you enjoyed the Sixpenny Cross series, please join Victoria and Joe in the bestselling, awardwinning Old Fools series. This true story and series starter is *Chickens, Mules and Two Old Fools*.

PREVIEW

1

THE FIVE YEAR PLAN

"Hello?"

"This is Kurt."

"Oh! Hello, Kurt. How are you?"

"I am vell. The papers you vill sign now. I haf made an appointment vith the Notary for you May 23rd, 12 o'clock."

"Right, I'll check the flights and..." but he had already hung up.

Kurt, our German estate agent, was the type of person one obeyed without question. So, on May 23rd, we found ourselves back in Spain, seated round a huge polished table in the Notary's office. Beside us sat our bank manager holding a briefcase stuffed with bank notes.

***

Nine months earlier, we had never met Kurt. Nine months earlier, Joe and I lived in an ordinary house, in an ordinary Sussex town. Nine months earlier we had ordinary jobs and expected an ordinary future.

Then, one dismal Sunday, I decided to change all that.

"...heavy showers are expected to last through the Bank Holiday weekend and into next week. Temperatures are struggling to reach 14 degrees..."

August, and the weather-girl was wearing a coat, sheltering under an umbrella. June had been wet, July wetter. I sighed, stabbing the 'off' button on the remote control before she could depress me further. Agh! Typical British weather.

My depression changed to frustration. The private thoughts that had been tormenting me so long returned. Why should we put up with it? Why not move? Why not live in my beloved Spain where the sun always shines?

I walked to the window. Raindrops like slug trails trickled down the windowpane. Steely clouds hung low, heavy with more rain, smothering the town. Sodden litter sat drowning in the gutter.

"Joe?" He was dozing, stretched out on the sofa, mouth slightly open. "Joe, I want to talk to you about something."

Poor Joe, my long-suffering husband. His gangly frame was sprawled out, newspaper slipping from his fingers. He was utterly relaxed, blissfully unaware that our lives were about to change course.

How different he looked in scruffy jeans

compared with his usual crisp uniform. But to me, whatever he wore, he was always the same, an officer and a gentleman. Nearing retirement from the Forces, I knew he was looking forward to a tension-free future, but the television weather-girl had galvanised me into action. The metaphorical bee in my bonnet would not be stilled. It buzzed and grew until it became a hornet demanding attention.

"Huh? What's the matter?" His words were blurred with sleep, his eyes still closed. Rain beat a tattoo on the window pane.

"Joe? Are you listening?"

"Uhuh…"

"When you retire, I want us to sell up and buy a house in Spain." Deep breath.

There. The bomb was dropped. I had finally admitted my longing. I wanted to abandon England with its ceaseless rain. I wanted to move permanently to Spain.

Sleep forgotten, Joe pulled himself upright, confusion in his blue eyes as he tried to read my expression.

"Vicky, what did you say just then?" he asked, squinting at me.

"I want to go and live in Spain."

"You can't be serious."

"Yes, I am."

Of course it wasn't just the rain. I had plenty of reasons, some vague, some more solid.

I presented my pitch carefully. Our children, adults now, were scattered round the world; Scotland, Australia and London. No grandchildren yet on the horizon and Joe only had a year before he retired. Then we would be free as birds to nest where we pleased.

And the cost of living in Spain would be so much lower. Council tax a fraction of what we usually paid, cheaper food, cheaper houses... The list went on.

Joe listened closely and I watched his reactions. Usually, *he* is the impetuous one, not me. But I was well aware that his retirement fantasy was being threatened. His dream of lounging all day in his dressing-gown, writing his book and diverting himself with the odd mathematical problem was being exploded.

"Hang on, Vicky, I thought we had it all planned? I thought you would do a few days of supply teaching if you wanted, while I start writing my book." Joe absentmindedly scratched his nether regions. For once I ignored his infuriating habit; I was in full flow.

"But imagine writing in Spain! Imagine sitting outside in the shade of a grapevine and writing your masterpiece."

Outside, windscreen wipers slapped as cars swept past, tyres sending up plumes of filthy water. Joe glanced out of the window at the driving rain and I sensed I had scored an important point.

"Why don't you write one of your famous lists?" he suggested, only half joking.

I am well known for my lists and records. Inheriting the record- keeping gene from my father, I can't help myself. I make a note of the weather every day, the temperature, the first snowdrop, the day the ants fly, the exchange rate of the euro, everything. I make shopping lists, separate ones for each shop. I make To Do lists and 'Joe, will you please' lists. I make packing lists before holidays. I even make lists of lists. My nickname at work was Schindler.

So I set to work and composed what I considered to be a killer pitch:

- Sunny weather
- Cheap houses
- Live in the country
- Miniscule council tax
- Friendly people
- Less crime
- No heating bills
- Cheap petrol
- Wonderful Spanish food
- Cheap wine and beer
- Could get satellite TV so you won't miss English football
- Much more laid-back life style
- Could afford house big enough for family and visitors to stay
- No TV licence
- Only short flight to UK

- Might live longer because Mediterranean diet is healthiest in the world

When I ran dry, I handed the list to Joe. He glanced at it and snorted.

"I'm going to make a coffee," he said, but he took my list with him. He was in the kitchen a long time.

When he came out, I looked up at him expectantly. He ignored me, snatched a pen and scribbled on the bottom of the list. Satisfied, he threw it on the table and left the room. I grabbed it and read his additions. He'd pressed so hard with the pen that he'd nearly gone through the paper.

Joe had written:

- CAN'T SPEAK SPANISH!
- TOO MANY FLIES!
- *MOVING HOUSE IS THE PITS!*

For weeks we debated, bouncing arguments for and against like a game of ping pong. Even when we weren't discussing it, the subject hung in the air between us, almost tangible. Then one day, (was it a coincidence that it was raining yet again?) Joe surprised me.

"Vicky, why don't you book us a holiday over Christmas, and we could just take a look."

The hug I gave him nearly crushed his ribs.

"Hang on!" he said, detaching himself and holding me at arm's length. "What I'm trying to say is, well, I'm willing to compromise."

"What do you mean, 'compromise'?"

"How about if we look on it as a five year plan? We don't sell this house, just rent it out. Okay, we could move to Spain, but not necessarily for ever. At the end of five years, we can make up our minds whether to come back to England or stay out there. I'm happy to try it for five years. What do you think?"

I turned it over in my mind. Move to Spain, but look on it as a sort of project? Actually, it seemed rather a good idea. In fact, a perfect compromise.

Joe was watching me. "Well? Agreed?"

"Agreed…" It was a victory of sorts. A Five Year Plan. Yes, I saw the sense in that. Anything could happen in five years.

"Well, go on, then. Book a holiday over Christmas and we'll take it from there."

So I logged onto the Internet and booked a two week holiday in Almería.

Why Almería? Well, we already knew the area quite well as this would be our fourth visit. And I considered this part of Andalucía to be perfect. Only two and a half hours flight from London, guaranteed sunshine, friendly people and jaw-dropping views. It ticked all my boxes. Joe agreed cautiously that the area could be ideal.

So the destination was decided, but what type of home in Spain would we want? Our budget was reduced because we weren't going to sell our English house. We'd have to find something cheap.

On previous visits, I'd hated all the houses we'd noticed in the resorts. Mass produced boxes on legoland estates, each identical, each characterless and overlooking the next. No, I knew what I really wanted: a house we could do up, with views and space, preferably in an unspoiled Spanish village.

Unlike Joe, I've always been obsessed with houses. I was the driving force and it was the hard climb up the English property ladder that allowed us even to contemplate moving abroad. In the past few years, we had bought a derelict house, improved and sold it, making a good profit. So we bought another and repeated the process. It was gruelling work. We both had other careers, but it was well worth the effort. Now we could afford to rent out our home in England and still buy a modest house in Spain.

"If we do decide to move out there," said Joe, "and we buy an old place to do up, it's not going to be like doing up houses in England. Everything's going to be different there."

How right he was.

Like a child, I yearned for that Christmas to come. I couldn't wait to set foot on Spanish soil again. We arrived, and although Christmas lights decorated the airport, it was warm enough to remove our jackets. Before long, we had found our hotel and settled in.

The next morning, we hired a little car. Joe, having finally accepted the inevitable, was happy to drive into the mountains in search of The House. We had two weeks to find it.

Yet again the mountains seduced us. The endless blue sky where birds of prey wheeled lazily. The neat orchards splashed with bright oranges and lemons. The secret, sleepy villages nestled into valleys. Even the roads, narrow, treacherous and winding, couldn't break the spell that Andalucía cast over us.

Daily, we drove through whitewashed villages where little old ladies dressed in black stopped sweeping their doorsteps to watch us pass. We waved at farmers working in their fields, the dry dust swirling in irritated clouds from their labours. We paused to allow goat-herds to pass with their flocks, the lead goat's bell clanging bossily as the herd followed, snatching mouthfuls of vegetation on the run.

Although we hadn't yet found The House, we were positive we'd found the area we wanted to live in.

One day we drove into a village that clung to the steep mountainside by its fingernails. We entered a bar that was buzzing with activity. It was busy and the air heavy with smoke. The white-aproned bartender looked us up and down and jerked his head in greeting. No smile, just a nod.

Joe found a rocky wooden table by the window with panoramic views and we settled ourselves, soaking in the atmosphere. Four old men played cards at the next table. A heated debate was taking place between another group. I caught the words 'Barcelona' and 'Real Madrid'. Most of the bar's customers were male.

Grumpy, the bartender, wiped his hands on his apron and approached our table, flicking off imaginary crumbs from the surface with the back of his hand. He had a splendid moustache which concealed any expression he may have had, and made communication difficult.

"Could we see the menu, please?" asked Joe in his best phrase book Spanish.

Grumpy shook his head and snorted. It seemed there was no menu.

"No importa," said Joe. "It doesn't matter."

Using a combination of sign language and impatient grunts, Grumpy took our order but our meal was destined to be a surprise. A basket of bread was slammed onto the table, followed by two plates of food. Garlic mushrooms - delicious. We cleaned our plates and leaned back, digesting our food and the surroundings. In typical Spanish fashion, the drinkers at the bar bellowed at each other as though every individual had profound hearing problems.

"We're running out of time," said Joe. "We can carry on gallivanting around the countryside, but we aren't going to find anything. I very much doubt we'll find a house this holiday."

Suddenly, clear as cut crystal, the English

words, "Oh, bugger! Where are my keys?" floated above the Spanish hubbub.

THE OLD FOOLS SERIES

Book #1

Chickens, Mules and Two Old Fools

If Joe and Vicky had known what relocating to a tiny mountain village in Andalucía would REALLY be like, they might have hesitated...

Book #2

Two Old Fools - Olé!

Vicky and Joe have finished fixing up their house and look forward to peaceful days enjoying their retirement. Then the fish van arrives, and instead of delivering fresh fish, disgorges the Ufarte family.

Book #3

Two Old Fools on a Camel

Reluctantly, Vicky and Joe leave Spain to work for a year in the Middle East. Incredibly, the Arab revolution erupted, throwing them into violent events that made world headlines.

New York Times top 10 bestseller three times

Book #4

Two Old Fools in Spain Again

Life refuses to stand still in tiny El Hoyo. Lola Ufarte's behaviour surprises nobody, but when a millionaire becomes a neighbour, the village turns into a battleground.

Book #5

Two Old Fools in Turmoil

When dark, sinister clouds loom, Victoria and Joe find themselves facing life-changing decisions. Happily, silver linings also abound. A fresh new face joins the cast of well-known characters but the return of a bad penny may be more than some can handle.

Book #6

Two Old Fools Down Under

When Vicky and Joe wave goodbye to their beloved Spanish village, they face their future in Australia with some trepidation. Now they must build a new life amongst strangers, snakes and spiders the size of saucers. Accompanied by their enthusiastic new puppy, Lola, adventures abound, both heartwarming and terrifying.

Book #7

Two Old Fools Fair Dinkum

Life is good. The grandchildren are thriving despite swallowing magnets and sticking crayons up their noses. But after a terrible drought, bushfire season arrives early, and flames rage across the land. Will love and laughter be enough to keep the Two Old Fools and their family safe from harm?

Book #8

Two Old Fools Find Their Tribe

One Young Fool in Dorset (PREQUEL)

This light and charming story is the delightful prequel to Victoria Twead's Old Fools series. Her childhood memories are vividly portrayed, leaving the reader chuckling and enjoying a warm sense of comfortable nostalgia.

One Young Fool in South Africa (PREQUEL)

Who is Joe Twead? What happened before Joe met Victoria and they moved to a crazy Spanish mountain village? Joe vividly paints his childhood memories despite constant heckling from Victoria at his elbow.

NEW! THE STILLWATER MURDERS BY VICTORIA TWEAD

DEAD OF NIGHT SERIES BOOK 1

Stillwater Cove is a town built on quiet.

When a string of unexplained deaths shatters the calm of Stillwater Cove, detective Lara Lennox is sent from Sydney to investigate. Each victim is found carefully posed, a small paper star left behind.

The Stillwater Murders (Chapter 1)

This is my time.
I am calm, but ready, prepared.

The dead of night, when the world exhales and falls utterly still. When darkness gathers like a velvet tide, drawn quietly over the earth. The sky becomes an ink-deep ocean without horizon or seam. A place where the stars seem to hesitate before shining. Even the gulls tuck their heads beneath their wings and stay quiet, surrendering to the dark.

There is a moment just before dawn, when the world forgets to breathe. The sea holds still. The reeds stop whispering.

I wait for that moment.

It is the best time a person can cross from this life to the next without struggle. Without fear. Without the burden of the weight of the world pressing in behind their ribs.

The old woman couldn't sleep. She sits on her veranda swing, wrapped in a faded, knitted shawl.

Her eyes are closed, her hair silvered by the moon.

I've been watching her. She didn't see me. I heard her trying to hum a tune she no longer remembered.

Her voice trembled.
Her hands trembled.
Her soul trembled.

But not now.

Now she is still. Perfectly still. Her heart no longer beats.

Now she is beautiful in her quietness.

I kneel beside her, careful not to disturb the blanket tucked around her knees. A faint night breeze lifts a strand of hair from her cheek, and I smooth it gently back into place.

Warm. Soft.

She earned this.

She carried her burden for so long that the weight bent her shoulders. No one noticed how tired she had become.

But I noticed. I always notice.

There is no fear in her face. Only the softness and peace that comes when the world finally releases you, lets you go.

I take the small, red paper star from my pocket.

It is imperfect. Torn by my fingers. A little crooked at the edges. The first star I ever made was for her, the woman who taught me how to say goodbye.

I place it gently under the old woman's hand, letting it rest on the shawl.

I breathe in.

A new beginning always starts with a quiet ending.

I stay with her until the light begins to rise behind the drowned forest.

Until the world remembers to breathe again.

Then I stand.

Gently close her eyes.

And leave her to her peace.

No one should die alone.

Amazon Link: https://bit.ly/Stillwater-Murders

REVIEWS

"I'm going: 'Nooooo! Don't go out, lock your door, don't let anyone in!' If this was TV I would be shouting at the screen."

"Totally wowed with it!"

"A brilliant edge-of-your-seat read."

"Totally and utterly gripping. I got nothing done while reading this."

NEW! THE BONE GARDEN BY VICTORIA TWEAD

DEAD OF NIGHT SERIES BOOK 2

THE BONE GARDEN

Some patterns should never be completed.

Bodies are turning up, posed with impossible care, surrounded by spirals built from bleached bones.

Detective Senior Constable Lara Lennox expects a straightforward hunt. Instead, she finds a killer who seems to know her team's next move before they do.

———————————————

DEAR FRAN, LOVE DULCIE

LIFE AND DEATH IN THE
HILLS AND HOLLOWS
OF BYGONE AUSTRALIA

Dear Fran, Love Dulcie is a true story, a rollercoaster read, with *an unguessable, astonishing ending*. It will inform you, surprise you, reduce you to tears and haunt you forever. I've never quite been the same since Dulcie's life touched mine. I'm deeply humbled to have been asked to put the story together for the world to enjoy.

"Shocking, yet heart-warming. Overwhelmingly

gripping." Beth Haslam, author of the Fat Dogs and French Estates series.

"Wow! Goosebumps." Elizabeth Moore, author of the Someday Travels series and Top 1000 Amazon reviewer.

"A truly remarkable young woman and a unique record of Australian life." Valerie Poore, author of Watery Ways.

"There are no words that can do this book justice." Julie Haigh, Top 1000 Amazon reviewer.

ABOUT THE AUTHOR

Victoria Twead is a New York Times, Wall Street Journal and Amazon bestselling author whose books span memoir, cosy mystery, psychological crime and children's fiction.

Her much-loved Old Fools memoir series was inspired by her years living in a remote Spanish mountain village, where she and her husband became accidental chicken farmers. She is also the creator of the charming Sixpenny Cross cosy mysteries, the darker, twist-filled Dead of Night crime series, and the delightful illustrated Mrs Arden children's books.

Victoria and Joe finally retired to Australia to watch their new grandchildren thrive amongst kangaroos and koalas. More joyous life-chapters are unwinding.

***

For photographs and additional unpublished material to accompany this book,
download the
Free Photo Book from
www.victoriatwead.com/free-stuff

CONTACTS AND LINKS

CONNECT WITH VICTORIA

Email: TopHen@VictoriaTwead.com (emails welcome)

Website: www.VictoriaTwead.com

Old Fools' Updates Signup: www.VictoriaTwead.com

This includes the latest Old Fools' news, free books, book recommendations, and recipe. Guaranteed spam-free and sent out every few months.

Free Stuff: http://www.victoriatwead.com/Free-Stuff/

Facebook: https://www.facebook.com/VictoriaTwead (friend requests welcome)

Instagram: @victoria.twead

Victoria's Cut-Price Paperback Bookstore: Books.by/Victoria-Twead

We Love Memoirs

Join me and other memoir authors and readers in the We Love Memoirs Facebook group, the friendliest group on Facebook.

www.facebook.com/groups/welovemem oirs/

VICTORIA'S BOOKSTORE

BOOKSTORE LINK:
BOOKS.BY/VICTORIA-TWEAD

If you prefer to read paperbacks, and would like to pay lower prices by buying direct, do visit Victoria's own cut-price bookstore. Shipping anywhere in the world is a flat fee of $5.

MORE ANT
PRESS MEMOIRS

AWESOME AUTHORS
~ AWESOME BOOKS

If you enjoyed this book, you may also enjoy these other Ant Press memoir authors.

All titles are available in ebook, paperback, hardback and large print editions from **Amazon**.

These two booksellers offer FREE delivery worldwide.
Blackwells.co.uk and Wordery.com
More Stores
Waterstones (Europe delivery), Booktopia (Australia), Barnes & Noble (USA), and all good bookstores.

VICTORIA TWEAD
New York Times bestselling author
The Old Fools series

1. Chickens, Mules and Two Old Fools
2 .Two Old Fools ~ Olé!
3. Two Old Fools on a Camel
4. Two Old Fools in Spain Again
5 .Two Old Fools in Turmoil
6. Two Old Fools Down Under
7. Two Old Fools Fair Dinkum
8. Two Old Fools Find their Tribe
9 .One Young Fool in Dorset (Prequel)
10. One Young Fool in South Africa (Prequel)

Dear Fran, Love Dulcie: Life and Death in the Hills and Hollows of Bygone Australia

BETH HASLAM
The Fat Dogs series

Fat Dogs and French Estates ~ Part I
Fat Dogs and French Estates ~ Part II
Fat Dogs and French Estates ~ Part III
Fat Dogs and French Estates ~ Part IV

Fat Dogs and French Estates ~ Part V
Fat Dogs and French Estates ~ Part VI
Fat Dogs and Welsh Estates ~ The Prequel
Fat Dogs: Beyond the Forest Fringe

DIANE ELLIOTT
Lady Goatherder series

Butting Heads in Spain: Lady Goatherder 1
El Maestro: Lady Goatherder 2

EJ BAUER
The Someday Travels series

1.From Moulin Rouge to Gaudi's City
2.From Gaudi's City to Granada's Red
Palace
3.From an Umbrian Farmhouse to Como's
Quiet Shores

For more information about stockists, Ant Press titles or how to publish with Ant Press, please visit our website or contact us by email.

WEBSITE: www.antpress.org

EMAIL: admin@antpress.org

www.ingramcontent.com/pod-product-compliance
Lightning Source LLC
Chambersburg PA
CBHW031018190726
48286CB00003BA/905